R00942 27335

T5-AOM-141

CHICAGO PUBLIC LIBRARY
LITERATURE AND LANGUAGE
400 S. STATE ST.   60605

THE CHICAGO PUBLIC LIBRARY
LITERATURE & LANGUAGE DIVISION

FORM 19   APR   1994

RANGE WAR

There was no way a man could stay on the fence in the hot, dusty little cowtown named Matador. The two biggest ranchers in the territory were feuding—and a man had to side with one faction or the other. Matt Carlin, a slow talker with a fast gun, was just passing through. He wanted no part of this mean war, but when a hired gunslinger threw down on him, he joined the other side just so they would know he couldn't be pushed.

RANGE WAR

Lee Floren

First published 1945
as *The Circle W*
by Phoenix Press

This hardback edition 1993
by Chivers Press
by arrangement with
Donald MacCampbell Inc.

ISBN 0 7451 4584 1

Copyright © 1945 by Phoenix Press
All rights reserved

British Library Cataloguing in Publication Data available

Printed and bound in Great Britain by
Redwood Books, Trowbridge, Wiltshire

ONE

MATT CARLIN WAS GOING DOWN the main street when the man spoke from the doorway of the saloon. He said, "Just a minute, fella. Just stand there and forget you own a gun. We don't need an Elwood gunman moving in on this."

Matt Carlin halted. He stood there, looking at the stranger, and he read him for what he was: a man who had seen a lot of country and who had seen some of the scenery through gunsmoke. Matt was tall and quiet, but the unrest was inside. Here it was again—he was just going toward the Matador Bar for a drink, and suddenly he was shoulder to shoulder again with trouble.

Matt said, "You got me wrong, fellow."

The narrowed eyes were sharp. "There's only two class of men on this Matador range, fellow," the low voice said. "Them that's for the Bar Y and old man Davis, and them that's with the Elwood Circle W. And you don't work for the Bar Y, because I'm on their payroll and I know every man."

"There's trouble?" asked Matt Carlin.

"Yes, there's trouble. But you knew that already. Just stand there and wait for a while, and don't reach for that gun."

Matt Carlin felt a great weariness. And mingled with this were the first faint stirrings of anger. He held this, though, storing it inside of him, but he wondered how long he would hold it. He let his eyes wander up the main street, this faint anger still in him, and he saw the young fellow who was just about ready to step into the buckboard, there in front of the Mercantile.

The stage is set, he thought. The kid has a gun on him, and probably he can use it, but the other fellow'll be faster, and he'll kill the kid. From what I gather, the kid's name will be Elwood, because this ranny just accused me of being an Elwood rider. That means that a Davis man will be stepping in soon, and then there will be gunsmoke... The pattern was old, and he had seen it before. Too many times, he realized.

The swinging doors of the Matador Bar, across the street from the buckboard, came open then and two men came out, and Matt Carlin saw that the killer brand was on them. One stood in the doorway and the other came out on the street. This man said, " Dave Elwood, I want to talk to you."

The first step, thought Matt Carlin. The first step toward murder. This fitted into the pattern, too, and it fitted well. The youth didn't have a chance, and Matt Carlin knew this, and he found it bothering him. This feeling was vague and remote, and he should not have had it, but it was in him just the same.

Dave Elwood turned, his hand on his holstered Colt. He was about twenty, Carlin saw, and he was a little pale, as though he had been out of the sun for some time. Matt Carlin saw him move back against the hind wheel of the buckboard and settle his back against this.

" What do you want, Lew Case ? "

" You've made fight talk against me," said Case. " Now back it up, Elwood, or crawl out of town with your belly dragging ! "

Dave Elwood looked at Lew Case. The other man—the one who stood in the doorway—had pulled back against the pillar, and he was watching carefully. Then he took his eyes from the pair and Matt Carlin saw he was looking at him and at the man who stood in the doorway—the man who had spoken to Matt.

" I got this one under control, Davis," said the man beside Matt.

This Davis was a big man, broad and heavy, and his jowls were thick. Matt almost felt the imprint of his eyes, and he felt the arrogance and power of their owner. Matt would have let the thing ride for what it was, but then Davis smiled a little, and Matt knew then he could not be neutral. For it was the smile that did it. It showed disregard and disrespect and contempt—and that drove Matt Carlin into action.

"Murder," he said quietly. "Murder out there on the street under that hot sun. This range deals in murder, I take it?"

"Watch yourself," warned the man.

Matt moved then, even as he had moved before, in similar situations. The pattern was old, therefore, and he executed it perfectly. He did not draw his gun. Bat Masterson and Tom Smith, to cite but two, had proven that the fist is faster than the gun, and Matt thought idly he would prove the old axiom again, even as these two old town-tamers had proved it twenty years before. He brought his right fist in fast, twisting his tall body as he moved, and he put his weight behind his knuckles. The man had his gun coming up, and then he saw the fist coming. For a moment, then, he found himself undecided whether to finish his draw or to throw up an arm for protection. He decided to do both, but the moment had passed, and the moment had been long enough for Matt Carlin.

He hit and he hit hard. The man went back against the building, and Matt Carlin came ahead, hitting four times. The man's eyes were not clear, and he flung out a right hand, taking that hand from his gun and letting it fall. He tried to go down, sliding with bent knees, but each time Matt hit him and brought him up, until Matt stepped back and let him fall.

Somebody said, "Hey, there's a fight down there! A stranger and Len Ducom, and Ducom's down, I tell you!"

Matt Carlin took Ducom's gun and threw it out into the street. The man lay on his side, his lips showing a touch of red, and he was unconscious. Matt turned and looked out on the street. This unexpected aside had broken the drama out there on the street and Lew Case had lost the feel of the act. People were moving across the boardwalk and coming toward Matt Carlin, and Lew Case looked up at Davis, who lifted his shoulders and pulled back his head.

Lew Case turned and went to Davis and they both went to Matt Carlin.

Davis asked, " What's up here, fellow ? "

" This man aimed to throw a gun on me," said Matt Carlin. " He had no cause to do that. I'm just a stranger passing through."

Davis nodded. He said, " He must have got you wrong, fellow. Probably figured you worked for the Elwood spread. You don't work there, then ? "

" No man's my boss," said Matt.

Davis said, " I see," and settled back. Lew Case was too quiet, and Matt Carlin glanced at him. Case's eyes were steady. Matt lifted his glance and looked at young Elwood, who had climbed up into his buckboard and pulled a rifle across his lap as he sat there. Matt felt the keen edge of impatience tug at him and he felt the silence and quietness of Lew Case and he knew the man was dangerous. He brought the thing to a point suddenly. He said, " You'd better get this man off the street, Davis."

Davis said, " Help Ducom into the Matador, Case." Case lifted the man, who was coming to, and another Davis man got on Ducom's left side, and they crossed the street with Ducom stumbling between them. Davis said, " I'll see you again, fellow. What did you say your name was ? "

" I didn't say," said Matt.

Davis was walking away. He turned and halted, and Matt saw that this man was strong, and that his strength was as tough as steel. He said, " You're getting off on the wrong boot, fellow."

" Just leave me alone," said Matt.

Davis said then, " I'd like to see you later."

" You won't if I see you first."

Davis said, " All right," and crossed the street and entered the Matador. Matt glanced at him and felt that unrest again. Somebody in the crowd said, " You made a dangerous enemy, fellow, and I'd walk easy in this town of Matador."

Matt Carlin said, " Thanks," and he said it dryly. Then he added, " But I won't be here long, just riding through."

He felt tired and a little sick and his knuckles hurt him. The old days had pulled up strongly and quickly on him and he did not want them, and this was no place to stay and he knew he would leave just as soon as he had eaten and had a drink of beer. By that time his sorrel would have felt the effect of hay and oats in the livery, and by morning he could be over the rim-rock and on a new stretch of land and by that time Matador would have only a faint memory of him and he would have almost forgotten the town and this incident.

"Ducom's gun is out there on the street," he said. "Somebody should pick it up; he might need it some time."

A townsman walked out and got the gun and Matt Carlin turned toward the sign that hung over a small log building down the street. He had lost some of his hunger; the trouble had caused that. Funny thing about trouble—when it came it pushed everything else away, even a man's physical needs. He had felt that before, too, and so he pushed it from his mind.

Dave Elwood said, "Stranger, I want to thank you."

Matt Carlin said, without stopping, "Don't thank me, fellow. Thank Ducom. If it hadn't been for him and his arrogance, I'd never have made that move. And thank Davis, too. He thinks any man will sell for money, I guess." He had seen that in Davis' glance.

"Wait a minute," said Elwood. "I want to talk to you."

Matt Carlin stopped. "What have we got to talk about, Elwood?"

"I could use a man like you on my ranch. The pay is one hundred dollars and——" He halted suddenly.

"And cartridges," finished Matt Carlin. "You don't intend to hire a cowhand, Elwood; you're hoping to hire a gunman. No thanks."

Elwood's thin face showed genuine regret. "Think it over; I'll be in town for an hour yet."

"Don't go gunning for Davis or Case," said Matt Carlin. "They'll kill you." He turned and walked away. He thought, I've said too damned much. If the button wants to get killed that's his business. To hell with the whole thing; I've seen enough of this to last me five lifetimes. The street was calm and the dust lay quietly in place and the sun was sharp and bright on it. You followed that trail and they put you away from the sun and you didn't see it again and it wouldn't make a bit of difference then whether the sun was warm and smooth or if there were rain and mist. He remembered the old Chimayo buck in New Mexico and how he had sat day after day outside his hogan in the sun, and how Matt had asked him why he liked the sun so much and the old man had said that for a long time to come he would be out of the sun. He remembered that clearly. Too clearly, perhaps.

"You ride for the C Bar C?" the old buck had asked brokenly as he looked at Matt Carlin's guns. "You have guns for the big ranch, huh?"

"I guess you'd call it that."

The toothless gums had parted in a smile. "Maybe then they put you away from the sun before they do me, huh?"

"Maybe so," Matt had agreed.

"You fool," said the buck.

Matt stopped in the doorway of the restaurant. From inside came the conglomerate smells of spice and ginger and the clean taste of steak and coffee. The sun was still bright out there, and it was warm and good. He took a stool and slowly read the menu. He toyed with the silverware and liked its cool touch. He ordered and rolled a cigarette and waited.

The Greek cook doubled as waiter. He put down the steak and spuds and said, "They're aiming to gun down young Dave Elwood." He was silent for a while, his wide forehead showing a scowl. "The kid needs help. His old man is dead—been dead about two years, I guess—and the fellow has a tough row——"

"Why tell me?" asked Matt coldly.

The Greek was puzzled. "You took up his fight."

Matt cut his steak. He held the fork in front of his mouth and looked up at the Greek. "An accident, brother, and nothing more. Ducom jumped me and I rile easy. Ducom knows that now. As for Dave Elwood, he can win, lose or draw. I'll be over the hill, and the one beyond that. You understand?"

"All right," said the Greek. "Forget it."

The Greek wiped the counter with his towel. Matt cut his steak and ate wordlessly. He was the only customer because of the hour. When he was almost through another customer entered, and he lifted his head and looked at her. She was about twenty-one or two, he reckoned, and what struck him first was her hair. He tried to find a colour for it, and finally decided it was bright bronze. Her Stetson hung across her back, the chin-strap against her throat, and the bright, bronze hair glistened under the light. She was pretty, too, he saw, but he decided she was not beautiful. Probably some rancher's daughter. She wore a loose silk blouse that did its best to hide her breasts, and her riding skirt was of finest unborn calfskin. Matt felt the imprint of her presence and held it as he returned to his meal.

The Greek said, " Hello, Miss Joyce."

" Hello, George." Her voice, Matt Carlin decided, fitted her personality: it was a trifle deep and husky, and held the lure of healthy young womanhood. " I'll take some iced tea, and that is all. Oh, maybe a cookie or two."

" Ride in with your father ? "

" Yes."

The Greek shuffled into the kitchen and the doors swung closed behind him. There was a short silence and then the girl said, " I'm Joyce Davis, mister. Hank Davis is my father. I'm sorry for what happened out there on the street."

Matt Carlin looked at her. Her eyes were blue and they held strength, a hint of Hank Davis' strength. He felt the pull of her presence, as any healthy man would have, and he thought nothing of it.

He said, " I'm just riding through."

" That's a good idea," she said.

Matt's glance was sharper now. " Why ? "

She shrugged. He found himself liking the gesture. It fitted her. " You couldn't sign up as a Davis hand after beating up Len Ducom. That would mean you would have to go over to Dave Elwood."

" No middle path ? " asked Matt.

" Not on Matador range," said Joyce Davis. " You're

either for or against Hank Davis in this country. There's no in between."

Matt asked suddenly, "Where do you stand?" He felt the silence grow up and take form and taste and substance. She was looking down on the counter top, tracing some pattern there on the smooth wood, and Matt found himself glancing at her finger. Her hands were small but yet they had a certain strength. Then the finger stopped and he cast his glance upward again and her face was the same as before. There had been something there when she had looked down, but that was gone now. What had it been?

"I'm my father's daughter," she said, and that was enough.

Matt nodded and continued eating. The Greek came with the iced tea, and Joyce Davis drank it slowly, but even at that she finished before Matt. When she left Matt glanced at her once, liking the looks of her pretty back, and he then leaned back and slowly rolled a cigarette.

"Good food well cooked," he said. "Been a long, long time since I had a meal that good."

The Greek smiled. He had a homely, lopsided smile which appeared strangely sharp on his broad, homely face. "Thanks, mister."

Matt stroked his match to life against his chaps and touched his Durham. When he got the cigarette drawing, he laid a dollar on the counter. "That cover the damages?"

"Jus' right," said the Greek.

Matt turned on the stool, one boot dropping to the floor preparatory to leaving, and the door opened and three men—Hank Davis, Lew Case and Len Ducom—came in. Matt stayed that way, the cigarette smoke idly twisting up, and he watched the three through it, something small and tight along his spine. Ducom looked at him, but he said nothing as he took a stool. Hank Davis was the first to speak.

"They tell me you've bought a half interest in Dave Elwood's Circle W," the cowman said. "Is that true, fellow?"

"What would I do with a cow outfit?" asked Matt

quietly. " Especially one that's set in the middle of hell with powder smoke ready to run across it ? " He twisted his cigarette and let it fall at his feet and he never raised his hands again : he left them with fingers spread out across his thighs and handy to his guns. Hank Davis saw this and read the gesture rightly. His eyes went small and tight and he seemed heavy with indecision. But when he spoke his voice was level and unhurried.

" You better ride out of Matador town, fellow, or one of us will have to kill you. That is, unless you hire out to my ranch and sling a gun for me."

Matt asked, " Is that a threat, Davis ? "

Davis was watching him very closely. His eyes, Matt saw, were without feeling; they looked dead, they looked lifeless. Matt looked at Lew Case, and saw that Case had grown dangerously quiet. Len Ducom pushed a little to one side, standing to the right of Davis, and Matt saw the hate that lay in his small eyes.

Davis said, " That's what it is, fellow ! "

Matt began thinking then, allowing his thoughts to run ahead, building and tearing apart the minutes, the seconds. But Davis did not know this, and he took it for uncertainty, for the beginning of fear. And therein he made his error. For Matt Carlin was thinking, There's no use trying to run away from it ; it catches up with you, and if you move on, sooner or later it overtakes you . . . Maybe the best thing to do is to stay and fight it and defeat the men and the guns against you, and maybe by making war you can find peace . . . Yes that must be it—there must have to be war before a man could find peace and the way he wanted to live his life.

He asked, " So young Elwood would like to sell part of his spread, huh ? " He did not wait for an answer. He got to his feet and went out the door and they stood watching him go toward the buckboard, there before the Mercantile. He went in and he saw Dave Elwood at the hardware counter buying a latigo strap.

Elwood turned and said, " Why, hello ! I thought you'd left town by now."

"They tell me you aim to sell part of your outfit," said Matt Carlin. "I'd like to look the place over; I've got a few thousand dollars I might invest in it. Why do you want to sell it?"

"I've been sick," said Elwood softly. "It's just too much to handle alone—that is, for a man in my physical condition. But, by gosh, I can't understand you—you claimed you were just riding on and you wouldn't take a job from me. Why, what happened, anyway?"

"Interest," said Matt Carlin. "Curiosity. Blame it all on that. Good as anything, ain't it, Elwood?"

Elwood was mystified and his thin face showed it. "I guess it is," he said. "Well, I'm leaving for the ranch right away. Tie him behind the buckboard and ride on the seat with me and I'll show you the country and my range. I think me and you would get along all right."

"I'll get my horse," said Matt.

The short rest had helped the sorrel, and Matt watered him again at the town trough. He walked up the street toward the buckboard, leading the sorrel. There was something inside of him, and he wondered if it were just the ironical, twisted thing called fate and nothing more. Then he lost this thought as he saw Hank Davis step out of the restaurant. Lew Case and Len Ducom came behind their boss, and the trio halted and looked at him.

"Walking out of town?" asked Davis.

"Just to Dave Elwood's buckboard," said Matt. "I aim to tie my horse behind it when we drive to the Elwood ranch in a few minutes. You see, Davis, I sorta took your hint. I'm looking over the Elwood ranch and I might buy a half share in it if I like the looks of the spread."

Davis' heavy face was impassive. Finally he said, "I see, fellow, I see." But the whole thing was too sudden, too piled-up for him, and Matt Carlin knew this. And he found himself smiling a little.

TWO

THE LEVEL LAND LAY SOUTH of the town of Matador. They drove along a thin road that ran its tortuous way to the south as it angled in and out of the *chamiso* and *yuccas*. The land ran out level like this for miles and then the foothills came out of the ground as though, suddenly disgusted with eternal flatness, they had lifted up in derision and anger just to break the serene levelness. They had lifted gradually, as though their wrath increased with distance, and finally their heights became tumbled, brush growths that had as their final culmination the high peaks of the Sangre de Madre range of mountains. The blood of the Mother Mary they were called because, if you looked close enough and were not too far away, you could see the red streaks of igneous boulders and sandstones that turned some parts of them into the colour of dark blood.

The summit of the Sangre de Madre range was about thirty some odd miles away, Matt Carlin knew. For, though he had never before been on this, the northern side of the mountains, he had been a number of times on the southern side, in Mexico. There were a few adobe towns over there on the Mexican desert that ran miles to the south, and a man could hole up over there and nobody would ever find him if he had a few pesos to slip the peons. Cristobal was one; there was Santa Margarita; and he remembered Guadalupe, too.

Dave Elwood said, " There's Hank Davis' outfit, the Bar Y. See it, over yonder on that plateau? You can just make out the buildings, it's that far away."

Matt Carlin followed the youth's pointing finger. They were in the higher country and he could see the ranch on a mesa to the west. The distance was about ten miles, at least, but the high Arizona air was clean and clear, and the buildings, though they looked small, were grouped around an organized plan, and not distorted and obscured by the heat waves of a lower altitude.

"Where does his range run?" asked Matt.

Again Dave Elwood's finger showed him. "That's Cottonwood Crick there; that's his south boundary. My Circle W line runs on the south of Cottonwood; his Bar Y travels along the north. You notice Cottonwood disappears down on the flat, don't you? Just runs into the sand and that's all. No more crick. No, I don't run on any of the level land; Hank Davis runs on it. My land takes up there and runs south and down to the border. See the summit of the Sangres? That's about where the international border runs, right along these peaks."

Matt Carlin found himself asking himself, Now what are they fighting over then? You only fight over two things on the open range, more or less. One is grass and the other is water. Davis holds the best grass and he has plenty of good water in Cottonwood. Elwood holds the poorer, hilly range and maybe he's forcing the fight . . . Maybe I ought to go light and look this over and maybe I'm on the wrong side of the corral at that. Then he sent out a feeler and asked aloud, "So Davis has plenty of water, huh?"

"Yes, he has."

Well, that didn't tell him anything. He asked, "And plenty of good grass, too, I see."

"Yeah, he's got good grass."

Matt Carlin leaned back against the buckboard seat and closed his eyes. Here, because of the altitude, the ground was cooling and therefore the air was cooler, and he felt it against his cheeks. He was going into something, and he wondered how big it was, and what it would come to end in. The rub of the leather cushion felt good against his back and he rode that way for some time, feeling the mountain coolness and the rising unrest. These fell to fighting in him and he let them struggle briefly, and then he pushed them down into limbo. He had the question on his tongue, ready to put it into words, and then he held it back, too. He'd find out what the fight was about later on.

He saw a few cattle that bore the Bar Y iron. They were a mixed up bunch of Mexican and Arizona stock. They were duns and buckskins and roans—these were Mexican cattle— and they had long legs and plenty of place to put the beef if they had had the grass. But they hadn't had the grass and therefore they were gaunt. Wide of horn, fleet of foot, they ran through the bush like deer, their horns back and heads pointed out as they broke through *chamiso* and *manzanita*. Most of the cows had calves and Matt Carlin noticed they were good calves, evidently sired by a good Hereford bull.

" You must have some Hereford bulls," he told Dave Elwood.

" I bought a couple of good ones three years ago in the livestock show in Tucson," said the young rancher. " The cows are throwing some good stock, too. See that two-year-old steer there ? He's got the bones of a Mexican cow and the meat of a Hereford. They make good rustlers and feed light and put on the beef. Though how a Hereford bull, slow as he is, ever catches one of those native cows, like they can run, is more than I can understand."

" How many head do you run ? "

" Around five-six thousand, I'd say."

Matt Carlin glanced at him curiously. " You don't know for sure, huh ? "

" Ain't had round-up this year yet."

A road-runner was travelling down the road ahead of the team. Matt Carlin watched the bird running along and thought, It's a hell of a cowman who doesn't know how many head he's got, and he's worse at the job if he hasn't branded his calf crop yet. Here it is late in July and those calves should be wearing the Circle W iron, because if they don't in a month or so they might be wearing somebody else's brand, and then they wouldn't be Dave Elwood's stock. There was something wrong here, and he wondered what it was. Well, if things didn't pan out right a man could always saddle up and ride over the hills.

" When the old man was alive he used to take close tab on the tally," said Dave Elwood.

Matt added that to his stock of information, and found the

B

sum to be exactly nothing. He wondered how the young man's father had died, and if that death had been peaceful. Or is any type of death peaceful, he asked himself. And now, with the old man dead, the son wasn't even bothering to round up and brand the spring calf crop. That didn't make sense. When you went into ranching you made your money from calves, and if you didn't brand them you didn't stay in the cow business very long. . . .

These thoughts were with Matt when they drove into the Circle W. They came upon the ranch buildings suddenly, turning the flank of a long, sharp hill and coming on the buildings strung along the base of a cliff. Here a canyon suddenly opened, shooting through the mountains, and lifting as it receded into space. Dave Elwood saw that Matt was looking at the canyon.

"Brush Canyon," explained the rancher. "That's the only canyon that leads over the Sangre de Madre range into Mexico. The rest run in a ways and end up sharp in box canyons. Anybody on this Matador range who wants to go to Mexico has to go through Brush Canyon." He added, "And I control the canyon."

"You sure could stop any rustling or smuggling both into this country and out of Mexico," said Matt.

Dave Elwood glanced at him sharply. "Yes, I sure could." He was silent as they drove into the yard. Four hound dogs came out barking at them. They were big, shaggy brutes, and Matt saw they were part wolfhound. Probably kept them for two reasons: to catch coyotes on the open range and to act as watch dogs. And they'd make good watch dogs.

Two riders stood beside the bunkhouse. They came forward as Matt and Dave Elwood stepped from the buggy. The old *mozo*, a gnarled, twisted, aged Mexican, led the team toward the barn.

One of the men was a tall, lanky man with shoe-button, arrogant eyes. The other was a bowlegged, homely son of the saddle. Matt saw that each packed a gun, and had that gun's holster tied down. They were gunmen and they seemed out of place in view of Dave Elwood's character, but then Matt remembered Hank Davis and his men and decided that Elwood, too, had hired some tough riders. Elwood introduced them to Matt.

The tall man was Jack Humphries. Matt felt his shoe-button eyes against his and read the man as a tough hombre. The other was Mack Williams.

"Jack Humphries is my foreman," said Elwood. "Williams here is one of my riders. Matt Carlin aims to buy in on the Circle W if he likes the looks of the spread."

Humphries looked at Elwood. "Figured you'd got over that idea of selling the cattle end of the Circle W, Dave."

Elwood shrugged. "If Matt's got the money to meet my price, I'll sell all my stock, Humphries."

Humphries nodded slowly. Something seemed to run between these men, and that something seemed to disagree with Jack Humphries. Matt too, was wondering a little: Elwood had said he'd sell *all his stock*. What then, if he disposed of his ranch, did he intend to do?

"The boys'll show you around, Matt," said Elwood. He turned to walk towards the house, and Jack Humphries said, "Zeke was here this afternoon, lookin' for you. Said he'd be back later, Dave."

Elwood stopped and turned. "What time was that?"

"About two, I'd say."

Elwood scowled. The gesture was definitely out of place on his thin, pale face. "Zeke shouldn't turn up in daylight," he said crossly. "No telling what the rangers have seen and where they're hiding. One of them might see him. When'll he be back?"

"To-night—some time."

"I'll be up to the house."

Elwood continued to the house. Matt untied his sorrel and led him into the barn. He filled the mow with wild mountain hay and filled it full, even tramping the hay down to get more in the place. Jack Humphries watched with a faint scowl.

"That hay was hard to get hold of, Carlin. Why not turn

your sorrel loose in the horse pasture with the rest of the saddle stock? He can graze out there just as well as eat hay here."

Matt said quietly, " When I need a horse, I need him handy, Humphries." He looked at Humphries suddenly and saw that the dark man was looking at Matt's guns, and he knew what Humphries was thinking.

" Okay," said Humphries, " okay."

Matt had the feeling suddenly that he was moving into something, and that it was dangerous. This spread he decided now, was no common cow outfit—for one thing, it didn't even brand its calves, and that meant it didn't make its living from cattle. Then how did Elwood make a go of things? A man needed money to foot a payroll, especially when some of the punchers were drawing gun-hand wages.

Matt had a hunch he should just keep on riding. But now, coupled with this, was a strong curiosity, and this struggled with common logic. Anyway he decided, he'd look the outfit over before pulling stakes. Dave Elwood's conversation with Jack Humphries had held a heap of curious statements. Such as the one about the rangers watching this man, Zeke, whoever he was. . . .

Matt toyed with that name, trying to hook it up to somebody he had either known or had heard about. But there was no tie-up in his mind, so he dismissed the thought. Humphries showed him an empty bunk in the bunkhouse. Matt tossed his duffel bag under it and stretched out full length, after washing at the pump to the back. He was tired, and the bed felt good under him, and he dozed off. The clanging of the cook's triangle brought him back to reality.

Shadows were gathering across the land, building up as the sun went lower behind the Sangre de Madre peaks. There was a chilliness, too: a chilliness you always find when you're high on the slopes of the southern mountains, in the rare, thin atmosphere. This bit through Matt's shoulder and made his skin tingle. When he entered the cook shack the Circle W hands were all seated, and he stood in the doorway and looked at them for a long moment. About ten riders, he saw, and again the thought came: How did Dave Elwood pay their wages when he didn't even take care to brand his crop of spring calves?

"Here's a seat," said Elwood.

Matt sat down beside the rancher. He was hungry and the meal was good. The Chink cook knew his cooking, and Matt ate with a slow deliberateness, fully enjoying the biscuits and coffee and roast beef. He wondered if Dave Elwood would introduce him to the assembled riders, but evidently Elwood either forgot or did not choose to, for it was only after the riders had left that the rancher spoke to Matt.

"Didn't ride around this afternoon and look the spread over, did you?"

Matt smiled. "Took it easy on my bunk. Reckon old age will be cuttin' me down still more right pronto." He added, "I'll do some riding tomorrow," and he got up. "I'll pour this cup, cook."

Elwood got to his feet and said, "I'll see you in the morning then," and went outside. Matt and the cook, a short Chinaman with a long queue, were alone in the cook shack. Matt poured his coffee slowly.

"Fellow around this outfit named Zeke?" he asked.

"No know," said the cook. He shrugged his skinny shoulders. "Me no know nothin'. By hell, all Goddamn it, China boy don't know nothin'. All hell, all Goddamn it, China boy don't want to know nothin'. China boy jus' cook, by hell."

Matt smiled. "What's your name?"

"Boys call me By Hell. Good name. Me like 'im!"

Matt finished his coffee. listening to By Hell scrape pans and talk under his breath. The talk was a mixture of Apache, Chinese and American, Matt decided. The whole thing was a jargon, running together and without meaning, and he pushed back his chair and went outside. The dusk had gathered and become the first darkness of night, and the lights from the bunkhouse and the house lay like rectangular sheets of flame across the cooling earth. He went to the bunkhouse and stood in the doorway for a while. Some of the hands were on their bunks, reading from tattered magazines or fixing personal gear, and four of them were playing cards on one bed. Matt counted them and saw only eight, and wondered where the others were. Then he understood : they were probably out on guard, somewhere along the trail that led to Brush Canyon. Matt went outside.

He felt uneasy, unsatisfied. Why he did not know; he probed into himself, trying to find the answer. He had no need to stay there, and if things didn't look right—if the range and water weren't what they would have to be to run cattle— he'd saddle up and head west and see what was doing over around Yuma. He walked to the corral and leaned against the bars and looked inside.

Three horses were in the enclosure. He watched them with a studied indifference, as though unmindful of their existence. They were wild broncs evidently waiting for the bronc-peeler to turn them into saddlestock, and they were shy of man and his smells.

One of them minced up toward Matt, walking lightly and suspiciously, and Matt remained still and quiet against the corral. The horse snorted softly, its curiosity aroused, and still Matt did not move. The horse did not quite understand this ; the men he had met before had chased him and caught him, and each time one of those men had hurt him. But this man made no move toward him. The horse nosed along the corral bar, sniffing at Matt's forearm. Matt shifted slightly.

The bronc stiffened and stepped back, alert suddenly. Then he was quiet for some time, the other horses watching him with pricked-up ears. When Matt did not move toward him, he pushed his nose forward again. This time he nuzzled against Matt's hand and Matt rubbed the soft nose with his fingers. The horse liked it and Matt cradled his nose in his hand.

The other broncs, wondering what the attraction was, crowded in a little bit, but fear kept them at a distance. Then they all wheeled suddenly and loped across the corral. Matt wondered what had caused their sudden fear. He looked behind him.

A person was coming toward him, coming out of a small

cabin to the west of the ranch house. Matt had noticed that cabin before, had seen the clean curtains on its clean windows, and wondered who lived there. Now he saw it was a girl. She was short, he saw; not any over five feet, if that tall. She wore a print housedress and her hair hung across her thin shoulders.

She said. " Hello."

Matt took off his Stetson. " Howdy, ma'am," he said.

The girl looked through the corral bars. " You were making friends with the horses," she said, " and they seemed to like it. I noticed one of them came up to you. Horses like you, don't they ? "

" Maybe that's because I treat them good," said Matt. He was studying her, noticed the dim lights play across the sheen of her dark yellow hair, and suddenly he found himself thinking of another girl, only this girl had bronze hair and was harder and had a brittle surface.

Matt said, " I'm Matt Carlin. I was drifting through and then I met Dave Elwood. I thought I'd look the place over and I might buy in on it."

" You'd buy into trouble," she told him.

Matt looked at her. " Why do you say that ? "

" Because Dave Elwood is my brother," she said quietly, " and I know Dave Elwood. He's dying on his feet, and he should be in his grave. You noticed it, I suppose. That low, deep cough and those bright spots on his cheekbones."

" Your name ? " asked Matt.

" Marjie."

Matt rolled a cigarette. He was stony quiet. Then he said, " You own half of this ranch, then, I suppose, Marjie ? "

She smiled. " Yes I do."

" Then if I did buy in, I'd have your permission, too ? "

She had her right hand on the corral bar. Now she brought her left up and put it beside her right, and Matt looked at her fingers. Her hands were short and chubby, and had no rings on them. He wondered why he thought of looking there for a ring . . . But a girl like this didn't stay on the marriage market very long.

"You have my permission," she said. "Any damn fool that would want to buy into gunsmoke——" She stopped suddenly. He saw her hands tremble a little. Then she let them drop to her side. "*Pardonme, senor,*" she said in soft Spanish, the liquid notes fitting her tongue and personality. "I hope I see you again—before you go? Will you grant me that?"

Matt wondered why she asked that. "Maybe I won't go, though."

"I think you will, Matt." She turned and went towards the cabin. Matt leaned against the corral, his eyes on her as she walked away, and he thought again of Joyce Davis, and and how straight she had walked down there in Matador. Marjie Elwood went inside and closed the door, and soon he saw the lamplight show in the windows of her cabin.

The bronc had come back, and he was nuzzling Matt's sleeve. Matt stroked his nose, but his thoughts were not on the animal. They were running and jamming up; he was rolling them over and trying to find something there; he was wondering what this was all about. There was danger here and danger rode the night air, and yet he didn't know what that danger was, and what constituted it. He looked up at the Sangre de Madres, limned against the darkening sky, as though to seek some knowledge from the crags. But they were as usual —heavy and tired and without thought, and without eyes and voice to tell of the countless times and countless men they had looked down upon during their lazy, sleepless centuries. . . .

He went to his bunk and to sleep.

THREE

THE MORNING WAS BRIGHT AND clear and a meadow lark sang somewhere on the lower reaches. Matt ate lazily and went outside. Riders were coming in and riding out, and some of them were in the bunkhouse, stripping down before going to bed. That meant there had been a night guard out.

He saw no sign of Marjie. The blinds, though were up in her cabin, and smoke lifted slowly through the chimney. He went to the barn, saddled his sorrel and was watering the animal at the trough when the man rode in.

He was short, squat, swarthy. A Mexican, Matt saw, and one of the tough ones; he carried two guns and a knife was stuck in his belt. His horse was leg-weary and marked by sweat and Matt saw he had been ridden all night.

" *A donde esta Dave Elwood* ? " he asked. He put the request into broken English. " Where ees Dave Elwood ? "

" Up at the house, I believe."

The Mexican looked at him through bloodshot eyes. " You new man here, no ? I no see you before, fella."

" New," said Matt.

The Mexican rode to the house, left his horse at the rack and went inside. Matt had read the brand on the horse and recognized it as a Mexican brand of a great *rancho* south on the desert, a *hacienda* noted for its tough riders. He tasted of this thought, and it was acrid and sharp.

The brief respite had strengthened the sorrel, and the gelding pulled at the bit. Matt rode the ridges and the foothills, looking for springs and waterholes back against the scarp of the Sangre de Madres. He scared a couple of deer from the *chamiso*. They were mule deer and big ones, and they galloped away on stiff prong-like legs. They went over a hogback, their tails dark and flat against their sleek rumps and disappeared in a deep gully.

There was a drift-fence cutting across the range at this point, and the enclosure must have been about forty some odd acres, he figured. This was choice range with long native grass and plenty of water. And he was somewhat surprised to see about a hundred head of burros grazing in the fenced-in grass.

He pulled in his horse and looked at the burros. They were short-legged, ludicrous beasts, and they lifted long, pointed ears and looked at him with calm eyes. He noticed that most of them had marks made by pack saddles and a few of them were still coated with grime and sweat, as though they had not yet rolled in the soft sand after being unsaddled. They regarded him owlishly and then fell back to grazing.

Now what are burros doing on this range? he asked himself. What did Dave Elwood and his riders have burros for, and what did they pack with them? He put the sorrel ahead, drifting down toward the lower reaches.

There were quite a few cattle on the range, and Dave Elwood had been right when he had estimated his herds at about five thousand head. But some of them were unbranded, and Matt wondered why no outsider had not branded them with his own iron. For it is an unwritten law on the range that when a calf quits sucking, if that calf is still unbranded, he is a maverick and belongs to the first man who puts a hot iron on him.

The sun came up and chased the mountain chill away. The grass was long and thick, and there was plenty of water. Here along the edges of the foothills, the pine and aspen and fir grew straight and in thick mottes. He came down a slant and reined in beside the small creek that tumbled noisily out of the rocks and the gully that ran deep into the foothills of the Sangre de Madres.

He leaned back hard against his cantle, the sorrel breathing heavily under him. Here would be an ideal spot to build a cabin. Yonder he could build the house, using the straight pines that grew back on the slope, the pines through which he could hear the sweet murmur of the wind. The creek would furnish water : clear, cold water. And the corrals could be built below the house on the clearing, and against the eastern slope a man could build a long low, barn.

He roused himself from these thoughts and rode down to Cottonwood Creek, the boundary between the Circle W and the Bar Y. The cattle were poor but this spring grass would soon put fat on them. Most of the cows were heavy with calves, and some already had their spring calves. They were mixed stock, but big stock, and the calves showed the blood of the Hereford bulls. And if Dave Elwood didn't want too much for the outfit, Dave Elwood had found a buyer.

He shifted in the saddle suddenly as a rider came out of the brush from across the creek. He saw that the rider was Joyce Davis, and his blood stirred slightly. She was riding a black and white pinto.

She called, " May I ride over ? "

Matt Carlin shrugged. He said, " *Bueno* with me."

She crossed the creek, her pinto's hoofs splashing silver spray. The water was only knee deep. She reined in and said, " Hello, there."

Matt said, " Hello."

" You're buying in on the Circle W, I hear."

" I might," said Matt.

" You're buying into danger," she said.

Matt stretched in the saddle. This girl's presence—her eyes, her bronze hair—affected him. He was quiet as he rolled a cigarette. He licked the smoke. " I've heard that before. Maybe I'm used to danger."

" Dave Elwood might sell you his cattle and range, because he has no use for either any longer. But he'll never sell the Circle W ranch house, nor he won't sell that pasture where he runs his burros, nor he won't sell Brush Canyon."

Matt asked, " Why not ? "

" He needs them. He needs them in his business."

Matt wondered what she was driving at. He decided to play along. He touched the sulphur to his cigarette. " I thought his business was running cattle."

" His business," said Joyce Davis, " is stealing cattle.

Stealing my dad's Bar Y stock, and stealing Lew Case's Heart Bar Nine cows."

Matt's brows lifted. " I thought Lew Case was your father's foreman. I didn't know he had a spread of his own."

" He proved up on some land down the creek a ways. He and Len Ducom own the outfit together. During slack season, they work for Dad."

Matt remembered Matador town. " They throw a sudden gun for him," he corrected her.

Her eyes showed anger. He liked them that way, he decided. She said, almost hotly, " All right, Carlin, walk into it. but keep a trigger handy, 'cause you'll need it. Dave Elwood is running cattle through Brush Canyon—our stock and Heart Bar Nine stock—and he's selling cattle to the revolutionists in Mexico. An army needs beef to fill its belly —even a nondescript, tattered Mexican army. He's running guns across too—or else how do you account for those burros ? "

Matt said, " Oh." He said it deliberately, lazily, as though unconcerned. And he saw her anger grow a little.

" You don't believe me ? "

Matt shrugged.

She was silent for some time. Finally she said, " All right, Matt Carlin, I just thought I'd tell you, that's all." She made to turn the pinto and he touched her reins. She drew up.

" That means then, Miss Davis, that you and I are to be enemies ? "

" What else could we be ? You'll own a part of a rustler's outfit, and you'll be stealing my father's cattle, my cattle."

" Maybe I won't buy in on the Circle W."

" That's your look-out."

Matt drew his hand back. He heard a rider across the creek. Lew Case was coming down the opposite bank, sliding a mouse-coloured buckskin through the wild rosebushes. He drew in, said, " You're on the wrong side of this crick, Joyce."

Joyce Davis said, " I'm over twenty-one, Lew."

Case rode across the creek. He rode slowly, deliberately.

His hand, Matt saw, was on his gun. He came in, leaned back in the saddle. "Better get on your side of the water, Miss Davis."

"You said that before." said Joyce.

Case looked at her, anger running across his eyes, and then he looked at Matt Carlin. Matt was smiling slightly, for this reminded him of a child disobeying a parent. Case saw that smile, and his anger solidified.

"Carlin," he said huskily, "you're ridin' into it, and you'll be carried out. You're signin' up with a rustler's spread, and the wages are lead and gunsmoke."

"Your advice," said Matt Carlin, "isn't worth a whoop in hell."

Case twisted in the saddle. The move was quick, swiftly executed, and Matt did not know whether he was drawing or not, for Case's body shielded his gun. Matt went on one stirrup, put his weight against the oxbow, and swung short and hard. The blow smashed Les Case on the jaw, and knocked him from the saddle. While Case's buckskin, snorting and frightened, trotted to one side, Matt dropped to the ground, his gun in his hand now. He heard Joyce Davis saying something, but he didn't know what it was; he paid no attention.

He said, "Forget you own a gun, Case!"

Case spat blood. He drew his gun hand back, braced it against the ground, shoved himself to his feet. He hunkered and spat again, and when he looked up his eyes were devoid of thought.

"All right, Carlin," he said.

His voice was too quiet, and Matt knew this: tides of anger were surging in the man, but they beat uselessly against the surface. And once again Matt Carlin read him for what he was: a dangerous man, more dangerous because of his quietness.

Joyce Davis said, "No more gun play, Carlin."

Matt looked up at her. She had a ·38 revolver on him. Evidently she carried the gun somewhere under her riding habit. He smiled and put his ·45 away. Lew Case got to his feet, went to his buckskin, and stepped up. Matt noticed he carefully kept his hand from the vicinity of his gun.

Matt said, " Good-bye."

Joyce answered, but Case was silent. The pair crossed the creek, climbed the far bank and rode across the foothills. Matt watched them for some time, remembering the quiet danger in Case's eyes, and he knew then that if he stayed on this Sangre de Madre range, he would eventually have to kill Lew Case. He was thinking of that when he met Marjie Elwood, about three miles away from the Circle W ranch house.

She said simply, " Thought I would ride out and meet you." Her grey fell into the pace. " How do you like the range ? "

" Fine range," he said. " The cattle, of course, are scrub stock, but the cows are having some big calves. There'll have to be some branding done, of course. How much do you and your brother want ? "

" Ten thousand, I think. You'd have to check with Dave."

Matt did some mental arithmetic. Five thousand head of cattle at ten thousand dollars, and a deed to patent land thrown in. He could raise that ; but it was dirt cheap, too cheap. And why ?

" Why such a low price ? "

She was looking straight ahead. " Dave's figures, Matt Carlin. Me, I'd never sell the ranch, never . . ." Her voice steadied. " But he won't sell Brush Canyon, or the ranch house and buildings, or the burro pasture. No, he needs them; he won't part with them. . . . "

Matt said, " So Joyce Davis just told me."

She turned suddenly, lithely, in her saddle, and looked at him. " Joyce told you that ? When ? "

He told her about meeting Joyce Davis and Lew Case, but he did not mention his trouble with Case. That, he decided, was his own business. They rode into the Circle W yard, the dogs barking, and Marjie rode to the barn where she unsaddled her horse. But Matt rode up to the ranch house and left his horse with dragging reins as he went to where Dave

Elwood was seated at a desk. Elwood looked up, the bright spots of his disease sharp on his thin cheekbones.

"You liked the range, Carlin?"

Matt nodded. "How much for all the cattle and the land?"

"Ten thousand."

"Cheap," said Matt. He added suddenly, "Why?"

Dave Elwood said, "T'hell with raising cattle; I'm through. I haven't got long to live, and I'm not going to fight wind and rain and sun during that time."

Matt looked at his fingers. "You aim to run beef across into Mexico, huh, and run guns across, too, with Zeke Pandrill?"

Elwood said, "Explain yourself, Carlin."

Matt felt suddenly tired, too tired. He said, "I got ears, Elwood, and I got eyes. I saw those burros. Pack Burros. Saw the sweat marks, the saddle marks, on them. I saw that Mexican come in this morning when I rode out. I didn't recognize him then, but it came back to me. He was with Zeke Pandrill one day, about six months ago, down below the Line in Santa Margarita."

"You've been around some," said Elwood.

"I know my way." Matt spoke in a low tone of voice. "No, Elwood, I don't want your spread." He leaned back in his chair, and let his thoughts run their course. This wasn't the place, and if he settled here it would mean trouble, and he didn't want any trouble. Marjie and Joyce and Lew Case and the whole bunch—Hank Davis and Len Ducom—they were all correct, and this was not the place for him. He'd pull one gun, and then he'd have to pull another, and the thing would add up and run up, and guns would settle it all. . . .

"It's this way, Matt," said Elwood. He got to his feet and walked to the window. When he turned, the spots had left his cheekbones. He looked like a boy now, as he had looked down there in Matador. Matt got the impression suddenly that this man was lost, that he was afraid of death, and that death was coming closer, day after day. And to fill the faulty spots in his character he was playing the game high, and playing it tough and rough. " You buy everything except the buildings, the burro pasture and Brush Canyon."

" And in return——? "

" Neither I, nor one of my gunmen, will touch your stock, Matt. I lift my hand to that, Matt."

Matt thought that over. He leaned back, seemingly relaxed and easy, yet tight and tense under his deceptive interior. No, it would add up the same—the causes had been planted, and they would bring about their effects with the passage of time, and this would bring smoke—gunsmoke. He shook his head.

" No dice, Dave Elwood." He got to his feet, his big rowels loud in the room. " Zeke Pandrill or one of his gunnies would step on my land, and then there would be hell to pay. I've met Zeke before." He didn't mention where and how that meeting, or those meetings, had occurred.

Dave Elwood said, " You're the boss, Matt."

Matt turned and went out. He rode to the bunkhouse where he had his blankets. He tied them behind his saddle. He was putting his boot in stirrup when Marjie came from her cabin.

" You're riding on ? "

Matt nodded.

" You're afraid, is that it, Carlin ? "

" No," said Matt, and then he added, " Just sensible."

Her voice was a trifle heavy. " You'll run then, and keep on drifting . . . You're like the rest of the men and most of the women too. You look for peace and quiet, and yet you don't seem to realize you have to fight for it ! "

Matt let his foot drop. He looked across the top of his saddle. Beyond the buildings lay the rolling, undulant foothills, marked by aspen and pine and *chamiso*. They lifted, they pitched—they became the mountains. And high on an alien peak, was a circling cloud, and the wind was howling up there, whipping against igneous rocks, snarling against scrub pine. . . .

Matt said softly, " You see a lot, Marjie."

She did not answer.

He stood there and looked at that cloud, at the mountain. Other winds were whipping too, inside of him, and the wind was cold, without mercy. He thought of that spot, down there on that nameless creek, and he thought of the straight pine that grew there. A man could build a house there.

Joyce Davis' hair was bronze—spun bronze—and her eyes were deep. And beside him, quietly thoughtful, was this girl who had hair of grey gold. He wondered why he thought of these two, and then he thought of that nameless creek again. He could hear it lapping against its banks ; he could hear the murmur of the wind in those tall pines.

He went into the house. Dave Elwood, still at the window, turned around. Matt said, " I'll buy the spread, Elwood."

" With the reservations I specified ? "

Matt nodded. " Even with those," he said.

FOUR

THE NEXT DAY MATT AND Dave Elwood rode into Matador together. Elwood was quiet on the long ride in, too quiet. Matt loafed in his kak, letting his thoughts run ahead, and finding little there for substance. This was a week-day and the little cow town was quiet, but when they racked their horses in the livery Matt saw that two Bar Y horses were there.

"Bar Y men," he said.

Dave Elwood nodded. "Hank Davis and Lew Case, I guess." He hitched his gun around, making the weapon ride ahead on his thigh.

Matt said, "For your own neck and for Marjie's sake—you shouldn't ride alone, Elwood."

Dave Elwood smiled and Matt saw the spots stand out against his cheeks. "A man can only live once, Carlin," he said. "I guess it don't make a damned bit of difference to anybody but himself if he happens to die. Some gents carry on and get religious and put all their bets on the next world, and all the time they don't know whether there is such a place. And as for Marjie, I reckon she can get along."

"Just a thought," murmured Matt.

Matador, although not the county seat, had a justice of the peace who had some county records, and Matt and Dave Elwood looked up the maps that showed the Circle W. The land, Matt found, was patented land—an old land-grant that had been purchased by Dave's great-grandfather from a Spanish *don*. The land was clear, too, with no mortgages or liens against it or the stock on it. With the help of the justice of the peace, they drew up a contract specifying the amount of cattle sold, the acreage, and holding the paragraphs that Dave Elwood would still retain ownership of the burro pasture, Brush Canyon and the Circle W *hacienda*. Satisfied, Matt wrote out a cheque on an El Paso bank, then signed the bill of sale and arranged with the justice to file it with the recorder at Tucson.

They went to the bank, where Dave Elwood told the clerk to put the cheque to his account. The clerk, a thin, elderly man, looked at the cheque for some time, until Matt said, " It's good, fellow."

" Pardon me," said the clerk quickly. " I wasn't doubting your signature, Mr. Carlin." He put the cheque in a drawer. " Thank you, Dave."

Matt understood, then. A great rancho was being sold—a proud Spanish land-grant—and it was going for a minor sum, and it was run-down and its cattle were unbranded, and its owner was riding a trail that led into Mexico . . . A far cry from that to its former greatness, when it was a raw and untamed land in a wilderness of Apaches and other marauders, both red-skinned and white.

They went outside. The sun was warm and clean, and Matt let it wash over him. Dave Elwood was coughing suddenly, low and deep into a red bandanna, and when the spasm passed he looked up at Matt, wiping the thin trace of blood from his lips.

" Bugs getting deeper every day," he said. He looked up at the noon-high sun. " Well, guess I'd better be hitting back for the outfit, Matt. You think you'll build down on Tumbling Creek, huh ? "

Matt nodded. " I'll see you."

Dave Elwood went to the livery barn, and Matt stood and watched him. Hank Davis and Lew Case came out of the hardware store, but Elwood was already riding out, heading for the Sangre de Madres. The pair crossed the street with Matt Carlin's watchful eyes on them and went into the Matador saloon. Matt stood and let his thoughts build up, and when he went toward the saloon Dave Elwood had ridden off into space, the folds of the foothills taking him from Matt's sight.

Hank Davis and Lew Case were still in the saloon. Case was drinking at the bar, and when he saw Matt enter—Case was looking in the back-bar mirror—he turned a little, and his eyes were cold. Hank Davis was leaning against the wall, looking down idly at a listless game of pinochle played by a few loafers. He looked up when Matt entered and said, " Hello, Carlin."

Matt said, " Hello, Davis." Case had turned and put his mug of beer on the bar, and he was watching Matt in the back-bar mirror. Matt met his gaze there and said, " Howdy, Case."

Case said finally. " *Bueno*, Carlin."

Matt said, " Everybody to the bar, men. I've just bought the Circle W Ranch."

The card players, glad for a wet respite, pushed back chairs and went up to the bar, with Hank Davis behind them. While the bartender shoved out glasses and bottles, Davis went against the bar beside Matt, and put one foot on the iron railing. He poured his drink with strong hands.

" So you're my neighbour now, huh, Carlin ? "

Matt said to the bartender, " Beer for me, fellow," and he looked at Lew Case. " What'll yours be, Case ? "

Case looked at him steadily. " Beer for me," he finally said.

Matt said, to Davis, " I bought the spread—all except the ranch *hacienda*, the burro pasture, and Brush Canyon."

Davis was ponderously silent, turning his whiskey glass with blunt fingers. He was watching the amber whiskey in deep thought. Matt had the impression suddenly that, though this man was tough, he was also fair. He was the kind of a man who would want to play square.

" So Dave Elwood kept those," he said. " That means, then, that he stays in this Sangre de Madre section and that the Bar Y keeps on losing stock."

The men along the bar were suddenly quiet. The silence grew up and became heavy, and Matt Carlin felt the sharpness of their eyes. Lew Case was dangerously quiet, turning his glass of beer slowly, studying the back-bar mirror to see Matt's reactions. Then the weight lifted when Matt said, " Neither me, nor my riders—when I get them—will harm the Bar Y stock, Davis."

The tension was broken, and the talk drifted back again.

"Where do you intend to build?" asked Hank Davis.

Matt told him that he would build on Tumbling Creek. Davis nodded, admitted it was a good place, but yet he was too quiet, too serious. Matt sensed this, and he knew what was bothering the big cowman : Elwood would still remain on this range, and there would be trouble, for Dave Elwood was with the border bunch. And he, a third party had moved in, and Davis did not know him very well—not well enough to know that his word was good.

"You'll have a hard time getting a crew," said Hank Davis. "Few men on this range, and those that are are working for either me or Dave Elwood. You can try, but I don't think you'll have much luck."

Matt found out later that the cowman had been right. For, though there were a few idle men in Matador, they did not want to work—they were saloon loafers and hangers-on, and had no taste for the saddle and the smell of a dawn fire. They made a little money around the bars by gambling and doing odd jobs, and they wanted their lives to continue in these same old familiar patterns.

George, the Greek cook, summed it up neatly that night when Matt ate in his restaurant. "They don't want to work. They ain't never worked, and they don't want to start now, Carlin."

Matt spent the night at the hotel. Caution implanted by the past days, coupled with this new danger, made him lock the door and put a chair against the knob on the inside, and keep the window closed with a low-pulled blind. When morning came he was restless and he ate a hurried breakfast at George's. A brief glance into the various saloons showed them almost deserted, and he knew it would be futile to look for riding hands in Matador.

He went to the hardware store and he ordered a wagon and some harnesses, and as many other things he would need as he could think of at the time. He also ordered saws and carpenter equipment and nails and other commodities necessary to construct his cabin and corrals. He met Joyce Davis on the sidewalk outside.

She said, " So you bought the Circle W, I understand."

He nodded.

She laughed a little. " Well, we'll be neighbours then, Mr. Carlin." Then, without warning, she said, " Dave Elwood gave you plenty of promises, I suppose. They sound good, Mr. Carlin ; very good. But Dave Elwood, unless you have already found out, is a liar, in addition to just being no good."

" I have suspicioned that," said Matt.

" Then," she said, " we agree on one thing, at least."

He said, " We could agree on other matters, too, I feel."

She did not colour. She looked at him, and he saw something in her eyes. It was not anger ; it was rather disgust. " I've heard that before, too," she said. " They all say that, and I thought you at least had originality enough to break the pattern."

He was slightly angry. He bowed. " Pardon me, Miss Davis," he said. His anger fell back.

She said, " I'm riding for the Bar Y. Would you care to accompany me ? "

" Thank you."

They went to the livery for their horses. The sorrel was gay, fresh from a night spent with a manger full of bluestem, and he pulled against the reins. Joyce Davis was riding a mouse-coloured buckskin, a smooth-walking, quick horse. The day was overcast with dark clouds over the Sangre de Madres, and this reflected its mood on them somewhat. They were, for the most part, silent but in the small talk that ensued, Matt got good glimpses into the girl's character, and he liked what he saw, and he wondered why. They parted at the fork of Cinders Creek. Joyce's eyes were without mirth.

" Ride a light saddle, Mr. Carlin."

Matt said, " I will, Miss Davis." The wind was raw and sharp now, coming down from the high snows, and a hint of rain rode its depths, bringing a freshness to it. The wind blew her hair slightly. He thought, A lovely girl and a girl a man could tie onto and never regret. . . . And he thought, too, of Marjie Elwood and her older, more sophisticated ways. She was bright against his mind : she was sharp and clear, and strangely disturbing. He sighed and shifted, and made his voice without feeling. " That I'll do."

" This will have to break soon," she said, almost disturbed. " The Bar Y is losing too many head ; if it isn't stopped soon it will break my dad. Men are riding these hills, and they've got rifles in their saddle holsters."

" You think Dave Elwood and his riders are stealing your stock ? "

" Who else would it be ? "

He thought then of Marjie Elwood. " I don't know," he said ; " I'm new here. Elwood riders are tough riders, and they ride fast horses." His smile was without mirth. " I know I wouldn't be able to hire them from Dave Elwood. And I know I wouldn't want them riding for my Circle W." He added, " I wonder if the Circle W has lost any beef ? "

" Would Elwood steal from himself ? "

Matt shrugged, smiled. " Just a question, Miss Davis." Rain was running across the hills toward them, and the first drops were hitting the dust. He had a picture of her, bright in his mind, when she said, " Good-bye," and turned the mouse-coloured buckskin toward the *rancho*, there on the high plateau. The wind was stronger, and the rain was hitting him as he untied his slicker. When the yellow oilskin slicker was across his shoulders, he let his sorrel drift with the wind and the rain, heading for the Circle W *hacienda*.

Strange thoughts were with him, and he rolled them mentally and pondered on the way of things. A few days before he had drifted into Matador. Now the drama was spreading, gaining in scope and intensity, and the future was falling into a pattern on him, and now they were past the stage of strangers ; they were becoming humans, and they had the faults and strength of other humans, and they had the pride and hate and the other human emotions that build up happiness and strife and hatred and conflict. They had backgrounds : they had assumed characteristics, had been clothed with an environment they were taking form and substance and, because of this, some of them were against him, and others were for him.

That, then, was the question, he told himself. The thing had gone far enough so that he could, at the present, know just who was his enemy, and who was his friend. Lew Case, of course, was against him ; so, for that matter, was Len Ducom. These two he was definite about, but the others would need time and space ; then, and only then, would each have his appropriate position on this mountain range.

Ahead of him and behind him and on each side of him there was this mist and rain. It was hitting his horse on the wethers and running off the bronc's rump. It slid from his oilskin slicker, dripped from the back of his Stetson. The rain was definite : it had taste, feel, còlour, size and dimension. This other had none of these ; they would be added later. Time would bring them.

The rain had fallen back somewhat when he reached Tumbling Creek. Evidently there had been a cloudburst back in the Sangre de Madres, for the creek was rolling madly between its boulders, churned by mud and sticks. The sorrel took the stream eagerly, splashing the muddy spray. A mile beyond that, he met Marjie Elwood.

He said, " You shouldn't be out in this rain, Miss Marjie."

" Good for the range," she said. " The air will be clean now, and the grass will be green. I guess it's God's way of cleaning the world. Maybe he's a big housekeeper, and his house is the world." She was smiling.

" Maybe so." He made his tone light. For he had glimsed something behind her seemingly irrelevant words, behind her smile. She had a front out, that was intended to trick the world, to make them believe she was happy. But behind this was worry, and he got a glimpse of it, and then it was gone, for she shifted to other things.

" Did you get a crew ? "

" No."

She hesitated. " I guess it is really none of my business. But just for a woman's curiosity, what do you intend to do for riders ? "

"Mexico. Santa Margarita, Guadalupe. Cristobal."

"Friends of yours?"

"They come to those towns—sometimes." He looked at her quickly. He knew what she was thinking: these were border towns and tough towns, and men came to them because they were that. "I'll probably need riders that know their way about."

"Yes," she said, almost too sharply. "With six-shooters. Well, the plot thickens, as the old melodramas used to say. I guess the rain is almost over with."

The rain had stopped by the time they reached the Circle W ranch house.

FIVE

LEW CASE AND HANK DAVIS reached the Bar Y at dusk. The sky was purple over the Sangre de Madres, and the colouring of blood ran across the high igneous rocks, once more giving them the hue that had named these peaks. Neither man had spoken much on the ride out, and Lew Case was quiet in his saddle. When Matt Carlin had bought the Circle W, another player had got into a speedy game—and Lew Case was wondering just what cards Matt Carlin held, and how good a player he would be.

They rode into the yard, and the old *mozo* came out of the barn and took the reins on Davis' horse as the cowman went down. But Case still sat his saddle, and Davis looked up at him.

"What's on your mind, Lew?"

"I ought to be getting over to my Heart Bar Nine," said Lew Case. Then, to the old *mozo*, "Is Len Ducom here?"

"He rode out this morning, right after you and Hank left. If I remember right, I heard somebody say he was heading for the Heart Bar Nine."

"Probably stay there tonight," said Case. He looked at Hank Davis. "Reckon I better mosey over that way, Hank, 'cause me an' Ducom want to do some work on our hoss corral come tomorrow."

Davis nodded. He went to the house, his rowels chiming in the evening. A chicken was scratching beside the barn, and idly Lew Case listened to its satisfied clucking. He turned his horse and rode toward his ranch. The dusk was growing thicker, and the mountain peaks were bright with the dying sun. The saffron of evening was spreading across the Matador range and turning to darkness. Lew Case did not ride fast; he let the horse hit a running-walk.

When he rode into the Heart Bar Nine the log ranch house was dark. The place was set on a flat expanse of land, and nobody could ride up without being seen. He pulled his horse in and hollered, "Hello, Len Ducom!"

Ducom said, from the house, "In here, Lew," and a lamp went into life, cutting a yellow hole through the one window on that side of the log structure. Case stepped down and led his horse into the adobe barn. The smell of rotting straw and horse manure was sharp against the mingled odours of the night and its vegetation outside.

He made out the dim outlines of a horse at the manger, and he settled back patiently against the wall, letting his eyes grow accustomed to the gloomy interior. Finally he recognized the horse as that of Ducom. There were no other horses in the barn, and Lew Case felt a touch of anger, for he had expected another horse to be there. He stripped his mount, took off his bridle, leaving only the hackamore on him, and tied the beast to a manger. He ran his hand into the manger, and it was empty.

"Damn that lazy Ducom," he said.

He got a four-tined hayfork and went outside to where the haystack was at the back in a wire enclosure. He took a big forkful and put it in the manger. When he entered the house, Ducom was sitting at the table, playing solitaire with a deck of greasy cards. He said, without looking up,

"What do you know, Lew?"

"Where's Zeke Pandrill?"

Ducom shrugged. "I got here about noon. He ain't showed up yet." For the first time he lifted lazy eyes. "You wouldn't expect the biggest gun-runner and cattle thief in Mexico to ride during daylight, would you, Lew?"

Lew Case was angry. "Hard telling what that damned fool would do."

The laziness left Ducom's eyes. He said, "Tell papa, Lew."

"Hank and I were down in Matador today. We saw this new gent, Matt Carlin. He just bought the Circle W from Dave Elwood."

Ducom leaned back in his chair. He was silent as he rolled a cigarette, but his blunt fingers spilled some of the tobacco. He got the smoke going and then looked up. " Where does Dave fit in ? "

" He kept control of three things. The *hacienda*. Brush Canyon, and the burro pasture. You know what that means, don't you ? "

" I'm not ignorant," said Ducom, " and I'm not deaf. That thickens the pudding, huh, and makes it harder to stir ? What do you see in the crystal ball, Lew ? "

Case said, " You got a drink ? "

" In the cupboard."

Case pounded across the pine floor. He took the bottle, wrenched the cork from it, and tipped it, drank, set it down. He came back to where Ducom sat and pounded the table.

" Carlin's tough ! But we got him on one thing—where will he get a crew ? He'll need men, and tough men, to run that outfit, to bust the brush and get those wild cattle out, and to brand them. And tough hands, too, to sling guns. 'Cause this whole thing adds up to one thing—gun-smoke ! "

" But where will he get that crew ? " asked Ducom. " No gunhands for hire in Matador, and Dave Elwood ain't paying his men—they're drawing wages from Zeke Pandrill. And with the high, easy money Zeke's paying them, they'll not hire out to a strange gent who'll pay them less and make them take half of their pay in bullets. . . . "

Case nodded.

Ducom said, " Rummy, Lew ? "

" I guess so," said Case. He went to the cupboard, got the bottle and two glasses, and sat opposite Ducom. " How did old Hank Davis take it ? " asked Ducom.

Case smiled. " All right with old Hank, I reckon. Matt Carlin said he'd run his outfit fair and square, and Hank took him at his word, I reckon. But we'll blast that, too, and when we get done Hank'll be gunning for Carlin, sure as hell. We got to keep these outfits fighting while me and you and Zeke set on the outside and rake in the profits and let them blame it on the other fellow."

"Could be done," said Ducom. "And easy enough too...."

The game ran on—a listless, lazy contest with neither man intent on winning, and each man marking time. A cow bawled out on the range somewhere and a calf answered the mother. The night was silent then, without wind and with only form and greyness, with the lamplight streaming through the window and pushing back the encroaching darkness.

Ducom finally said, "Maybe Zeke ain't coming, Lew."

"He said tonight," said Lew Case.

Ducom shuffled the cards. His fingers, despite their shortness and bluntness, worked easily, surely and quickly. He flicked the cards out rapidly, making them wink in the lamplight.

"You should have been a gambler, Ducom."

"A millionaire's son would have been better, Lew." The man leaned back and yawned. "Wish that damned Mex would get here." He drew a card, glanced at it, tossed it into discard. "Rio de Janeiro's a big town. I've seen pictures of that beach curling along the cut of those mountains."

"Dream some more," said Lew Case.

"I'll be there," said Ducom. He rubbed his jaw. "That is, unless Matt Carlin hits me again, like he did down in Matador." He grinned across the table at Case. "How does your jaw feel, Lew?"

"You talk like a damned——" Case stopped, listened. Somewhere a horse was moving, coming closer. Then the sound of the hoofs fell back and died. "Must be Zeke now, huh?"

"Who else would it be?"

Case sat there, rubbing his thin nose, and Ducom leaned back, tall and lean in his chair. Time ran out and the minutes lengthened. Case's hand came down, falling to his gun, and he felt the raw rub of waiting. And when Zeke

Pandrill entered he did not come through the front door; they heard his boots in the kitchen and both turned, waiting.

Zeke Pandrill said, " *Como esta hombres !* "

He was in the doorway then, a short, thin man. His face was heavy, almost too wide for his slender build, and his thick lips showed a smile. A bandolier ran across his buckskin-clad shoulders and he wore an old ·45 tied low on his left hip, the grip protruding to the front. From his Yaqui forebears he had inherited sleek, dark eyes. The dark skin was donated by his Spanish ancestors. From his Irish father he had inherited a sparkling smoothness, a glibness of tongue. But, with all these, he was dangerous, and the border country knew this.

" You wait for me, no ? " He did not wait for an answer. " Sometime, when you leave the shade up like that, a man creep through the night and fire through the window—and you will be dead, *senores*. . . . "

Lew Case went to the window and pulled the blind low. " Left it up so you could look inside and see who was here, Zeke."

Ducom pushed his chair back. " Dave Elwood sold the Circle W cattle to Matt Carlin," he said. He looked sharply at the outlaw.

But the outlaw showed no surprise. " Dave told me this morning," he told them. " Jack Humphries and Mack Williams ain't here yet, huh ? "

Lew Case said, " They should be along pronto." He turned from the window. His long face bleak. " Matt Carlin'll watch Circle W cattle, Zeke. He won't be as easy to deal with as Dave Elwood. But so far he can't hire any riders——"

Zeke Pandrill took a chair, pulled it back against the wall, then sat down. He could watch both doors into the room. " He can hire a crew," he said. " He knows a number of men, some of them on the shady side of the law, and he's got plenty of friends. Carlin hasn't ridden a straight trail, and he's used his gun a number of times, but the law has no charge against him."

Case looked at him, surprised. "You know him then, huh?"

Zeke Pandrill nodded. "A little."

Riders were somewhere in the night, and a horse's hoof clashed against a stone. Lew Case moved to the back door and stepped out into the night as the two riders came in at a long lope. They left their mounts in front and Lew Case came back into the house. "Humphries and Williams," he said.

"Come in," said Zeke Pandrill.

Jack Humphries' shoe-button eyes swept over the trio. They were sharp and keen, and quick in their judgment. Slouchy Mack Williams hooked a chair, pulled it in, and sat down. Humphries moved to the right a foot or two, then settled on his haunches, his back against the rough wall.

Zeke Pandrill asked, "Did you ride over from the Circle W?"

Humphries looked at him. "We come from Ada," he said. "The guns are over there, and Pancho and Rigo are loading them on the pack mules. Carson got them in the same way—wagon train. The mules'll make Whinton Springs by morning, hole up there in the timber until tomorrow night; then we shove them through Brush Canyon."

Zeke Pandrill's stubby brown fingers rolled a corn-husk cigarette loaded with native uncured Mexican tobacco. Ada was a mining post and Carson, the trader, brought in supplies and, with these, smuggled in rifles for the Mexican revolutionists. Now another burro-train would go across the border. Zeke Pandrill blew a lazy cloud of smoke, thinking of that.

"See any sign of rangers?"

Humphries said, "Not a sign, Zeke."

The renegade Apache looked lazily at the others. "Any of you others see any rangers?"

Lew Case shook his head. Ducom said, "No." Mack Williams shrugged, let his shoulder fall. But Zeke Pandrill's wide, dark forehead sported a deep scowl.

"Maybe we got the wrong turn on this ranger deal,"

he finally said, " but we better keep our eyes open and our mouths shut." He looked at Humphries and Williams. " I suppose that you boys know that Dave Elwood sold the Circle W iron and stock and range to this Carlin gent, didn't you ? "

" Figured he would," said Humphries.

Lew Case felt a stirring of impatience. " All right," he said suddenly, " let's get down and look at this bronc's hoofs, men. Zeke, just where does Matt Carlin fit in, and what do you aim to do with him ? "

The renegade's cigarette was breaking. He ran his red tongue along the seams of the corn-husk and slowly fitted it together. When he looked up, his eyes were scheming.

" We run guns just the same, of course. We steal Bar Y cattle like we've always done. We tote the guns into Mexico and sell them ; we drive the stock through and sell them."

" We know that ! " Case's tone was rimmed with impatience. " Sure, we'll do that, just like we always have. But how about Circle W cows ? Are we still going to steal cows with that iron, like we used to steal them off'n Dave Elwood ? "

" Seems odd that Elwood never got wise to us stealin' his iron," said Jack Humphries. " Good luck Brush Canyon sets four or five miles back of the Circle W *hacienda*, like it does, or we'd never be able to run Elwood's brand into the canyon."

Case said angrily, " Why bring that up, Jack ? That's old and buried. Dave Elwood has to stay close to the house nights or else the night air raises hell with his lungs." The Bar Y man looked again at Zeke Pandrill. " Are we still stealin' Circle W cows since Matt Carlin got the iron ? "

The Yaqui showed in Zeke Pandrill's slow eyes. " There are two ways to do this," he said quietly. " One is to get both the Bar Y and Matt Carlin down our necks. We don't want to do that, of course. The other is to get the Bar Y and Matt Carlin fighting. That's what we want. Because while they're scrapping, we're stealing both outfit's cattle."

" All right," said Case. " What's next ? "

"Don't rush me," murmured Zeke Pandrill. He was silent for a moment, and Lew Case felt the bite of the silence, as did every man in that room. "Carlin hasn't got all his stock branded. That'll be his first chore. While he's roundin' up one side of his range, we'll steal from the other."

"But how about Hank Davis?"

"What if Davis branded a few head of Carlin's calves, and those calves—with Davis' Bar Y on them—are sucking Carlin Circle W cows?"

Case leaned back. "Easy to do," he admitted. "Just run the Bay Y on some Carlin calves, and when Carlin sees it he'll jump old Hank Davis' frame and there'll be a ruckus, and if I'm there I'll try to change it into a gun ruckus."

"Do that," said Pandrill. He was quiet then, and he felt fatigue rush in on him. The ride across the Sangre de Madres had been high and chilly with a smart wind, and he had not slept for many hours. "If we got that all settled, I'd like to hit the hay, Case."

"There's a bunk in the end room," said Case. "Me and Ducom'll stay here tonight and head for the Bar Y come morning."

Zeke Pandrill looked at Humphries and Williams.

"We'll head into the Circle W," said Humphries. "Dave Elwood thinks we went out on the north side of the foothills to look at some water holes. You cutting Elwood in on this rifle deal this time, Zeke?"

"Not unless he finds out about the guns going through," said Zeke Pandrill.

Humphries said, "More for us, then . . ." and went outside with Mack Williams following. Zeke Pandrill listened to their hoofs die out there in the night; he was tired and discontent. He sat there for some time, his chair tilted against the wall. Finally Case and Ducom left the room, going to their bunks in the room across the hall. Still Zeke Pandrill sat there, squat and yellow in the lamplight. An hour went by and then he stirred, getting to his feet. He walked to the lamp and blew it out and darkness held the room.

He went down the hall, walking slowly. When he reached his room he jacked a chair under the knob—nobody could enter—and he went to the door that led out into the *patio*. He opened it and looked out into the night. The moon was coming up and the range was showing shadows and colour.

There was a high, small window in the 'dobe wall. He got on a chair, opened it, then took a piece of spot cord from the corner. He tied this around the knob of the back door and tied the free end to a chair beside his bed. If that door were opened during the night, the chair would slide across the floor and wake him up. He put his Colt under his pillow.

Only then did he go to bed.

SIX

Marjie said good night and went to her cabin. Matt Carlin unsaddled his sorrel and the girl's buckskin and turned the buckskin into the pasture but put the sorrel in the barn, making sure that the manger was full of hay. He had noticed, when riding past the burro pasture, that it had been empty.

The burros were in the barn, munching hay. And Matt knew that a shipment of contraband was going through Brush Canyon that night. The smugglers would strip the saddles and packs from the tired burros and transfer them to these fresh beasts, then go into Mexico.

Matt went to the Circle W *hacienda*. The rain was coming back a little, moving down from the Sangre de Madres, and the lash of it stung his face. He entered without knocking. A kerosene lamp was turned low on the table. Evidently Dave Elwood had gone to bed. Matt decided to go down to the bunkhouse and hit his blankets. But Dave Elwood had heard him enter. His voice came from down the hall.

" I'm in bed," he said. " Is that you, Marjie ? "

" It's me, Matt Carlin."

" Come on in," said Elwood. " Have a drink, Carlin."

Elwood had on a lounging robe. He lay on the bed. He was coughing when Carlin entered ; coughing deeply, almost silently. Matt Carlin stood and looked at him and felt a strange pity for this man. It was the pity that a strong man holds for a sick man he knows will have to die soon.

The spasm passed. " Where's Marjie ? "

" She rode in with me," said Matt. " She went to her cabin."

Elwood had a whiskey bottle on a bedstand. " You want a drink, Carlin ? "

" No."

Elwood was a little drunk. He showed it now. " You afraid of my bugs ? " he challenged. " Is that why you won't drink with me Carlin ? "

Matt said quietly, " I never drink whiskey, Dave. Don't like the stuff." He felt a little restless ; he did not like this room and this man who would die soon.

Elwood looked at him. " How were the burros out in the pasture when you rode in ? I suppose they were standing under the oaks and cottonwoods to keep out of the rain, huh ? They should be in the barn on a night like this."

Matt thought, There's something wrong here—the burros are in the barn and he doesn't know it. Then he doesn't know there is going to be a smuggling pack-train going through. That means, then, that Zeke Pandrill is double-crossing him.

He said, " They were probably back off the trail under the oaks. It was getting pretty dark when we came in, Elwood."

Elwood yawned. " I'm sleepy."

Matt left. He went outside to go to the bunk-house. On the the outside porch he met Marjie. She still wore her slicker and her yellow hair glistened in the lamplight coming through the window.

" Where's Dave ? "

Matt said, " He's in bed. He's been drinking. He wanted to go to sleep, so I left him." He glanced at Elwood's window. The lamp inside the sick man's room went out suddenly. " He just put out his light."

She sat on the railing, her back against a pillar. The rain was running slowly off the eaves and it dripped from the porch roof. The light from inside framed her and showed that she was tired.

" That lamplight," she said. " It hurts my eyes."

Matt went back into the house and blew out the lamp. then he came back on the porch and stood beside the girl, who leaned back against the wide pillar, her eyes closed. neither of them spoke. Matt watched her, entirely too aware of her magnetism, feeling the strong pull of her personality.

" What does the doctor say ? " he asked.

"He might die tonight, and he might live for a long time yet. This high climate, he said, was a little too cold at nights for him, and he wants me to get him into Mexico and out on the desert. But what can I do, Matt? He seems intent on dying, and I guess there is nothing I can do about that, is there?"

"No, I guess not."

She said, "The burros are in the barn. Did he know they were there?"

"No. He asked me if they were in the pasture. I told him they were. That means that Zeke Pandrill is double-crossing him and running guns across without cutting him in on it. How does Pandrill get by with that? Why don't some of the Circle W riders tell your brother?"

"They're on Pandrill's payroll."

"I see," murmured Matt Carlin. Things were falling into place and the puzzle was getting form and pattern, and he was learning the answers to some of the questions he had asked himself when coming to this high mountain rancho. "Are you going to tell him?"

She shrugged. The gesture fitted her. "And what would he do? He'd get his guns and he'd challenge Pandrill, and the Mexican would kill him. No, he'll live a little while this way, going on in ignorance of Pandrill's deceit, but if he found it out it would mean his death, for if Pandrill didn't kill him then one of Pandrill's men would."

"Then I've broke up this whole play?" he asked.

Her eyes were serious. "Why do you say that?"

He tried to keep his voice from being too bitter. "I buy the Circle W Ranch. It's right in the middle of outlaw territory. Sooner or later Pandrill will enroach on my property. When he does, I'll go for my iron and kill him. Is that why you asked me to stay on this range? Did you want to use me against Pandrill for the profit of you and your brother?"

Her voice was low. "Don't say that, Matt."

"Then why did you ask me?"

She leaned her head back and looked up at him, her hair spilling across the yellow slicker. The wind had risen and it was singing quietly in the eaves. "My father owned this *rancho* and before him his father owned it, Matt. They fought for their lands, their herds, their families. Then along comes this miscast of the Elwoods, my brother, and he is weak and he starts to lose something I and my people have held for centuries. . . . "

Matt understood then.

" You're strong," she said. " You've got—well, you're a wolf, and these others are just coyotes, and you'll whip them. What good will this do me ? None." She shrugged again. " I've lost the ranch now and the Elwood line is broken up. Maybe this is the way a heroine talks in a story book, but it's the truth. Your hands are strong and they'll build the Circle W back to its old strength."

She talked quietly, simply. She did not reach out and touch his hand braced against the porch railing. He was glad for that. She was appealing to him through logic, not through physical attraction.

" What do you plan to do now ? "

" Get Dave talked into going into Mexico. Get him away from Pandrill and his renegades. Get him to spend what little time he has left in peace and not cursing the God that made him and gave him breath."

" But what will that hold for you ? "

" That's the least I can do, isn't it ? "

Mat said, " I guess so."

She got to her feet. She said, " Good night," and went to her cabin. Matt saw the door open, saw her body limned against the lamplight, and then the door closed. He had seen a part of her life, an intimate part, and now that part was shut away from him, cutting her thoughts from his as the door shut her from his sight.

The wind was sharper now, whistling a little, shrill and bitter as it came from the Sangre de Madres. The bite of it was coming through his slicker, but he paid it no heed, listening to the rustle of men and gear down by the barn. He turned and looked at Dave Elwood's window but it was still dark ; inside the man slept in a sick and drunken sleep. He did not hear the sounds beside the barn.

Matt reached for his gun and pulled it ahead, moving the belt on his hips until one of the ·45s rode in his middle, the grip sticking up. This way if needs be, he could reach it easily through the open front of his oilskin. He went down to where the men stood beside the barn.

Jack Humphries was there and so was Mack Williams. Altogether, about seven or eight riders stood in the group. Humphries' black eyes were glistening points behind the coal of his cigarette.

He said, "Thought you'd be in the bunkhouse asleep, Carlin."

Matt Carlin rolled a cigarette. He did not need the smoke, but he wanted to see the bunch in the light of the match. Three of them were Mexicans, and he looked hard at one before the flame died.

"I've met you before," he said. "What's your name?"

"Gomez."

Matt nodded. He broke the match, flipped it away. "Down in Juarez," he said. "I remember now." He tried something. "You want a job riding for me?"

"Got job."

Matt looked at Humphries. "You want to ramrod my outfit?"

Humphries said stiffly, "No." Then he added, "You should get to your bunk, Carlin; this night wind is cold."

"I guess I can stand it if you can," said Matt. He curbed his rising antagonism. "When does Zeke Pandrill and his burro train come in?"

There was a rigid silence. "You know quite a bit," said Humphries. "Can you add, too, Carlin?"

Matt Carlin stepped forward. He grabbed the front of Humphries' heavy shirt, reaching through the man's open slicker. He twisted and the cloth tore a little, then held. Humphries was going for his gun but he was having difficulty getting his hand under his slicker. Matt brought his other hand up, the knuckles tight, and hit Humphries under the jaw, knocking him back against the wall.

Matt swung round, his hand on his gun. Humphries

cursed and spat blood. Williams' hand was reaching under his raincoat. The others stood motionless, wondering just what was next.

Matt said clearly, " Take your paw from that gun, Williams, or I'll kill you ! "

Williams drew his hand back.

Matt looked at Humphries. " That's just a sample of what you'll get if you get tough with me. I bought the Circle W range and if I catch you putting a horse on it, or a boot on it, I'm using a rifle or six-gun, whichever is the handier. I figured you might just as well learn that now as later, Humphries. That goes for you, too, Mack Williams. *Sabe?* "

Williams said, "*Si*," and was silent.

Humphries' eyes were clearing. " I guess——" he began, then halted as they heard a rider coming up through the darkness. He was riding a dark horse, a tired horse ; he was on them almost before they saw him, and Matt recognized him.

Zeke Pandrill said, " Got things ready here, men ? The burros are just behind me a quarter-mile or so. We better get through Brush Canyon before the rangers—Where's Dave Elwood ? "

" In the house," said Matt. " In a drunken sleep. Your little double-cross deal will work okay, Pandrill."

Pandrill came down off his horse. He said, " Now who the hell are you ? " and then he stopped in his tracks. He stood there, short and thin, bold in the night, and he looked at Matt.

" Well, Matt Carlin, no ? I hear about you buying this ranch. We meet again a little, huh ? "

Matt nodded.

Zeke Pandrill looked at Jack Humphries. " What happened, huh ? "

" He talks big," said Humphries, " and he acts big to back up his tongue. But the next time he won't catch me napping, Zeke ! "

Matt moved to one side, his hand still on his gun. " We'll get to the core of this, Zeke. You know me and I know you . . . we've met before, as you say. I own this Circle W range. You got your way to make dinero and I got mine. I don't give a damn if yours is dishonest or not."

"*Si?*"

"You leave me alone and I'll leave you alone."

Zeke Pandrill nodded his swarthy head slowly. "Fair enough, Carlin. But thees Dave Elwood, you no tell him about this gun-train to-night?"

"None of my business," said Matt. "You just stay off my property and we'll get along all right. But if I see one of your men on my land I'm running him off or killing him, whichever is the handier."

Pandrill nodded again. "*Si.*" He turned to his riders. "Here comes the burros, *hombres*. Work fast and without noise." His men went into the barn and the Mexican renegade looked at Matt. "There is trouble ahead for us, Carlin."

"Not unless you or your men make it," said Matt.

SEVEN

MATT WENT TO THE BUNKhouse, where he lay for hours, listening to the singing of the wind against the roof. Many thoughts plagued him and sought for answers. Of only a few things he was certain, and these brought no assurance to him. He had four enemies on the Sangre de Madre range, and all of those enemies were deadly. He reviewed them mentally.

Lew Case was one, and Case would only wait for the right time and place. Len Ducom was the second, and he was like Case; they were two of a kind, and that was why they ran together. Jack Humphries was another, and Humphries, too, was dangerous. But of the quartet, Zeke Pandrill was the most deadly.

Pandrill and he had met before, riding on either side of some range or wire-cutters' fracas, and each appreciated the other's ambitions and character. Pandrill was deadly and Pandrill was smart. And now he had bought a ranch in the Sangre de Madres and Pandrill ran guns and contraband through Brush Canyon. That, in itself, would lead to disaster—not that the running of guns into Mexico was any of Matt Carlin's business. But the fact still remained that Zeke Pandrill was on that range and that sooner or later their trails and ambitions would cross. And when that time came, only gunsmoke could settle the argument.

For he knew this: Pandrill was cunning and his stubbornness matched his cunning. And that stubbornness would cause the border bandit to reach for his weapon. He had seen this flaw in Pandrill's makeup before, and he knew it was the renegade's chief weakness.

Sleep was slow in coming. Across the screen of his mind moved many figures and many thoughts. The last few days, jumbled and kaleidoscopic as they had been, had, nevertheless, held the high spicy taste of danger. New people had moved into those thoughts and had given them range and scope and brightness. Hank Davis, grumbling, swearing. And then, too, there was Joyce Davis. There was a flash of bronze-gold hair, a brightness and gayness, the slow smile that showed the white teeth, the frown that brought the lines to her tanned forehead. He thought of her, and wondered at his thoughts, and then let them slip into limbo.

Contrasted with Joyce's brightness was the sombre, reliable character of Marjie Elwood. Her hair was golden and her smile was slow and meaningful. She had taken a trail that would lead her far from the path her life should have chosen, but fate and destiny had driven her to that, and her high sense of duty, because of filial ties, demanded that she stay with her brother.

Rain was falling again, beating on the roof. That rain, he knew, would muffle all sounds of the burro train as it left. And in the big house, Dave Elwood would be sleeping, unmindful of the deceit, the trickery that was passing him and moving into Brush Canyon. He would sleep the way a boy sleeps: his right arm under his head, lying on his right side. But it would not be the peaceful sleep of a healthy boy. His would be the sodden, drunken sleep of a whiskey-saturated man—a man who would never feel the sharp, invigorating sting of the wind in clean lungs, a man to whom each breath consciously drew him that much nearer to death. . . .

He dozed off then, and came awake later. He awoke suddenly and he was aware, first, that the rain had ceased and the wind had abated. Then he understood what had awakened him. Men were moving into the bunkhouse and were undressing on their bunks, and he knew then that the smugglers had run the train through and had come home.

"Hell of a night," he heard a man grumble.

"What gets me," said Jack Humphries, "is where are these damned rangers? Or is that all hokum we keep hearing, that about the Arizona rangers moving in on this district? Nobody's seen one yet."

"Maybe this Carlin gent's a ranger."

Humphries laugh was low. " You ought to talk with Zeke Pandrill, Williams. He'll give you some words on this Carlin gent."

" Carlin's in his bunk," said a man quietly.

Matt Carlin had his eyes seemingly closed. Yet, through the small slits of his eyelids, he was watching Jack Humphries. Humphries glanced at him and said, " Good place for him," and crawled between his sougans. " Remember, now, everybody get up usual time and eat, just like we'd been here all night, and then Dave Elwood'll think we been asleep all night."

" His sister," said Mack Williams, " she gets me, Jack. Why don't she tell Dave about us double-crossing him ? She knows, sure as hell."

" Lots of things get you," said Humphries. " You take it easy, Mack. Hit that pillow and keep your lip sewed tight."

There was no sleep for Carlin after that. He got out of bed before dawn, dressed silently, went to the cook-house. By Hell, swearing mundanely, was stirring the fire, cursing at the coffee, the weather, and life in general. His slitted eyes lighted when he saw Matt Carlin.

" By hell," he jabbered. " All hell cold out, by hell. By Hell get you some cloffee, huh, no ? "

Matt ate and went outside. Dawn was lifting a red hand over the Sangre de Madres. He went to the barn, where he saddled his sorrel and rode south, heading into Brush Canyon. The wind was moving strongly across the hills, but when he entered the canyon the rise of the walls on either side cut the wind off and made only a ripple of current swinging down the cut toward Mexico. He rode slowly, letting the sorrel pick his own pace.

The canyon ran into the heart of the Sangre de Madres and finally lifted up and ended on a high mesa. Here the wind whistled and howled through scrub pine and dwarf cedar. The ground had been hard all this distance and the rain had washed away almost all the hoofprints of the burros. only here and there had Matt seen the spore of the smuggler's pack-train.

This mesa, he figured, was the International Border. From there the slopes became less fierce and ran down into the Mexican desert to the south. This vast sink was below him, marked by ocotillo and cacti and sand, an endless blue dish of land that ran miles and miles towards the equator and finally became lost in the distance. Over it rode the deep, impotent sky that looked down on this desolation and wilderness without emotion or thought, and which had gazed down on it centuries before man came to mar the sand by his insignificant footprints.

He brought his gaze in and looked for Cristobal but he could not see the town, for the high folds of the foothills hid the sleepy adobe Mexican village. Evidently the rain had not been so much on this side of the divide, for here he saw the tracks of the burros clearly. All the tracks he saw ran towards Cristobal, and he could not see any return tracks. Thst meant that the burros had been left in Mexico to be taken back some other dark night when they were not so tired and leg-weary.

A deep ravine ran down toward the south and he put his sorrel down it. Ten miles farther on his memory found various landmarks and, though he had been in this country but a few times before, he recognized these and knew then how close he was to Cristobal. A few minutes later, when he rounded a bend in the ravine, he saw the desert suddenly spill out before him, and there was Cristobal.

A meandering, yellow main street, seemingly tired and looking for some shade, angled crookedly, the shadows of the 'dobe buildings falling across its dusty surface. A few Mexican kids were playing where the sidewalks would have been had there been any, and they looked at him and said, "*Americano! Americano!*"

He had a few coins in his pocket. He tossed them to the children. They scrambled madly for them. "*Gracias, Americano, Gracias.*"

He swung down in front of the *Catina del Oro*, leaving the sorrel with his reins dragging, and he went inside the cool saloon. The floor was hard packed earth, beaten into compactness by high-heeled boots and moccasins. The bartender, a gross, sloppy man, was sitting on a stool, looking at his hands. He glanced up when Matt entered, held him in his dark eyes for a moment, then let his gaze drop.

Matt said, " Beer, señor."

" *Si.*" The obese man waddled to the well at one end of the *cantina*. He pulled up on a rope and soon a bucket filled with beer bottles came to the surface. " What kind you want, no ? "

" *Tecate* beer."

The fat man waddled back, uncorked the bottle. " They have *Tecate* beer in El Paso, huh ? "

" No." Matt drank. He didn't want the beer but that was an opening wedge to conversation. " I've been here before, Pablo. You remember, huh ? "

The black eyes surveyed him closely. " Your face, she ees familiar, no ? But yet I cannot remember too well. Sometimes I forget fast, huh ? "

" Good idea." The beer was cool. Matt lowered the bottle. " Have you seen Joe Hawkins around here lately ? "

" Don't know him, what's his name—huh ? Joe Hawkins ? You want to see him, no ? "

Matt smiled. Pablo knew well enough ; he was playing it close. And Matt didn't blame him ; any man would have in Pablo's occupation and position. " When you see Joe Hawkins, tell him I want to see him. Tell him to get five good men and come up north across the line. He'll find me at the Circle W outfit."

" You buy that outfit, huh ? I hear about it a while ago. Then you are Matt Carlin, I guess, no ? "

" You know me," said Matt, grinning. " Don't act so dumb, Pablo."

Pablo shrugged. " I no know nothings, señor. But if I see a man named Joe Hawkins, I tell him to ride to your place. You want 'nother beer, huh ? Good *Tecate* beer ? "

" *No mas, gracias.*"

Matt went outside. He leaned back against the 'dobe, feeling the heat against his back, and looked up and down the main street as he rolled a cigarette. Pablo should have admitted he knew him, yet Pablo hadn't done that. He rolled that slowly in his mind, enjoying the bite of the sun after the cold morning ride, and tried to find some answer to that thought.

Two vaquaros came out of the *Morales Cantina*, at the end of the block, mounted and rode past him at a long trot, hitting for some ranch that lay along the southern base of the Sangre de Madres, and as they cantered past they nodded to him and spoke. Matt lifted his hand, let it fall. He did not know them. But here, on the southern rim of the border, men spoke to one another whether they knew each other or not. Matt swung his thoughts back to Pablo.

Pablo would get word to Joe Hawkins and Joe would come. And when he came, he would bring riders—gun-riders. This conflict was growing larger and more concrete; it was getting feel and taste and colour. Word would go from mouth to mouth, and wherever Joe Hawkins was he would eventually hear this word, and he would ride across the border.

Matt pulled back into the alley. He went down the littered, sun-baked strip, stepped into the back door of the *Morales Cantina*. The transition from bright sunlight into semi-darkness had the normal effect on his eyes, but he moved forward to the bar to where two men stood drinking. They heard his boots on the packed 'dobe floor and they turned.

Matt came up to the bar and said, " Howdy, Case. Howdy, Ducom."

Case grunted, " Hello, Carlin."

Ducom did not greet him. " You're a distance from home, Carlin," he said gruffly.

Matt Carlin looked at him steadily. " I could say the same for you, Ducom. What are you doing in Cristobal ? "

Ducom became stiffer. " That tongue of yours will get a bullet through your brisket for you, Carlin."

" You won't send it there."

Case said, almost too quietly, " Damn it, Ducom, take that chip off your shoulder ! " Then, to Matt, " Drink, Carlin ? "

" Beer."

Matt poured the amber liquid into a dirty glass. He said, " To Matador range—with the hope of fat cattle and good calf-gathers and peace." He lowered his glass. The tension was high and he deliberately increased it. " I came over here to hire a crew."

" Mexican ? " asked Case.

Matt shook his head. He regarded his beer idly. " *Gringos*," he said.

Ducom said, " No *gringo* riders in this town, Carlin."

" That's right," said Matt. " There are none now, but they can ride in, Ducom." His inference was clear.

" Gun-riders," murmured Lew Case. " More hell on Matador range." He turned veiled, unmotivated eyes lazily on Matt Carlin. " A man with the t.b. eating out his lungs, a Mexican bandit and raider, gun-hung riders on good horseflesh, cattle and three outfits now—yes, and two women, beautiful women." His smile was twisted. " The ingredients of a flock of hell, Carlin."

" No need to stir it," said Matt. " I ride a straight trail— if you leave me alone, Case." He turned slightly as the bat-winged front door opened. An American came in, a big, heavy man of about fifty. He wore battered, worn range trappings and his face was a heavy mass on heavy shoulders. He stopped, looked at Case and Ducom, then at Matt Carlin.

" Hello, Carlin," he said.

" Drink, Johnson ? " asked Carlin. He had not seen the cattle buyer for two or three years, and he wondered what the bluff Scandinavian was doing on that side of the line. " You move around. Last time I saw you was in Juarez, I believe."

" I get around," said Johnson. He ordered tequila with a beer chaser. " Never expected to see you around Cristobal, though."

Matt Carlin told the cattle buyer that he had bought the Circle W. He watched the man closely, trying to read the effect of the information on the heavy, dour face, but if the words had any effect on Hans Johnson, the man did not show it. Carlin asked him if he knew Case and Ducom and the cattle buyer said he didn't, so he introduced them.

Johnson nodded to them. Matt Carlin was quietly reserved, feeling the thing out, and he had a sudden hunch that these men had met before and they didn't want him to know that fact. He downed his beer and said, " Well, I better be moseying along, men. See you later."

Case and Ducom grunted something indistinguishable. Hans Johnson said, " So long, Matt," and Matt went outside. He walked to his horse and stepped up and rode down the street heading north. No horses stood at hitchracks and he rode up to the long, low ' dobe barn on the outskirts. He dismounted in front of the water trough that ran along the front of the building to the west of the door. A wiry Mexican was dozing there in the sunlight.

" You put your *caballo* in my barn, huh ? "

" Sit still," said Matt. " I'm just giving him a drink." The Mexican settled back, pulling his straw sombrero over his eyes. Matt moved to one side and glanced through the open door into the barn.

Three horses were inside. One, he figured, belonged to Hans Johnson, but the others, he saw, were Heart Bar Nine broncs. The horses were dry and had been curried. That meant that Case and Ducom had been in town for some time. Matt wondered when they had ridden in but he knew it would be useless to ask the hostler. That worthy, like the rest of Cristobal's citizens, would be close of mouth because he lived in Cristobal.

But he did know that, wherever Hans Johnson went, there were cattle for sale. And, knowing the cow buyer, he knew that Johnson did not care what brand those cattle were, just so he could turn them over and make a profit on them. Matt had a lot of mental fodder, and he chewed it thoroughly. Maybe Case and Ducom had some Heart Bar Nine cows for sale and wanted to sell them hot across the border to make more on them. Or maybe they were selling cows that belonged to somebody else. . . .

E

EIGHT

By noon, Joyce Davis had reached the higher land, her palomino gelding sweaty from the long, hard climb. Bar Y cattle had been grazing the length of Cottonwood Creek, and none, so far as she could determine, had crossed the stream onto Matt Carlin's Circle W. She pulled the palomono in and let him breathe and she looked over the rolling, undulant range below her.

Finally she sent the horse downslope, forded Cottonwood Creek and rode out on Circle W land. She swung south and east, cutting across the edge of the Heart Bar Nine, and headed toward Tumbling Creek. The sun was warm and the muscles of the palomino lithe and limber and she loped along, swinging the free end of her catch-rope that was tied to the fork of her saddle.

She looked back once, wondering if Lew Case or Len Ducom were following her, but she saw no sign of her two bodyguards. The thought of the two brought a frown to her forehead and she wondered whether her father had asked the two to protect her or if they had taken the chore on themselves. She had asked Hank Davis and he had grumbled something that had sounded like, "You ask the damnedest questions," and that was all she could get out of him. Hank Davis was a gruff gent, and now he seemed worried—too worried, she thought.

She almost rode over the man. He was sitting beside the trail, his back to a rock, and he was eating his lunch. He lowered the sandwich and stared up at her as she drew in her palomino. He was a stranger to her, and then she remembered she was on Circle W range.

She said, "Hello."

"Howdy, ma'am." He did not take off his Stetson. He was a heavy man with a thick-jowled, enormous head that was set on beefy shoulders. He was the type that did not work for a living, she decided. "You must ride fast, miss. Right before I started to eat my lunch I was up on a hill and I couldn't see a rider anywhere."

"Is Matt Carlin home?"

"I don't know, ma'am. You see, I don't ride for Carlin, whoever he is. I'm just a stranger riding through and thought I'd light here awhile to rest my horse and eat my lunch."

Joyce glanced at his horse. The sorrel cropped grass indifferently a few rods away, tied to a boulder with a catch-rope. The horse did not look as if he had been ridden far nor was he very hungry. Had he been hungry, he would have been grazing faster than he was.

"Oh," she said. Her first shock of the meeting had passed. She had the impression that the man wished they had not met but she was not sure. "*Adios.*" She turned and rode back toward Tumbling Creek again. When she gained the opposite ridge she glanced back but the horse and rider were gone. She saw them later when they reached the flats, and they were going toward the hills to the north-west.

The hills grew steeper and the pine grew thicker. On these higher slopes the wind was a little stronger—too strong, she thought. It caught her bronzed hair and pulled it back and she let it blow in the breeze. She was on the wrong range and she knew it, and she told herself she should not have come, and yet all the time she realized that her mental reproaches were without avail.

But when she rode down the slope toward the cabin being constructed below, she wished suddenly, more than ever before, that she had not come, for as she rode in she saw the grey horse tied to an aspen tree and she recognized the horse as a Circle W horse, Marjie Elwood's favourite mount. But it was too late to retreat, so she pulled in before Marjie and Matt Carlin, who had been working on the door frame in the log cabin that stood about shoulder high to Matt.

"Hello," she said.

"Hello," said Matt. He rubbed his shirt sleeve across his sweaty forehead. "Step down and rest your saddle, Miss Davis."

"Yes, do," Marjie invited her.

Joyce Davis dismounted and let her palomino stand with dragging bridle-reins. She was stiffly polite as she asked, "How are you, Marjie?"

"Fine," said Marjie. She looked at Matt. "Shall we go on working on this door frame?"

"We'll finish it," said Matt. "That'll be all I do for today."

While Marjie held a pine board in place, Matt sent in the nails. Joyce sent a cursory glance around the yard. She decided that Matt Carlin had been really working. In a week he had constructed an emergency barn and laid the groundwork for a log cabin. A fence on Tumbling Creek held some saddle horses and a team of work horses. A wagon, its bed covered by spools of barbed wire, a canvas tarp and other ranching necessities, stood beside the barn, a set of harness hanging over one side of it. He had even built a small pine-pole corral.

"You've been working," she said.

Matt mumbled through the nails in his mouth. "A little." He drove in the last nail, spit those out between his lips, tossed them into a barrel of nails, tossed the hammer in on top of them. "Thanks, Marjie."

Joyce Davis thought, He's calling her Marjie, not Miss Elwood. She asked, "How is your brother, Marjie?"

"The same, I guess," said Marjie. "Sick, Joyce."

"Tell him hello for me."

"I will," She added slowly, "But I don't know how he would take it—your father and Lew Case tried to murder him one day down on Matador's main street."

"Oh," said Joyce stiffly.

Matt Carlin said, "By the time you get to your place it will be dark, Marjie. Thanks a lot for the help."

Marjie Elwood untied her grey and found the stirrup. She turned the horse. "Good-bye, Joyce," and then to Matt,

"I'll probably see you tomorrow, Matt." She neck-reined the grey around and rode off.

Joyce Davis said, " I could break her neck ! "

Matt Carlin smiled. " Is that all you women ever think of, hating each other ? What have you two got between you ? She doesn't own the Circle W iron any longer ; I do."

"Oh, yes," said Joyce, a little too sweetly. "We were raised together on the range, Matt Carlin. We went to the same country school together. We know each other very well. All right, I'll say I'm sorry. But I'm not."

Matt looked at her sharply. He liked what he saw. "What are you doing on Circle W range ? " he asked.

She shrugged. " We're neighbours, Carlin." She glanced at his cabin, at the barn, at the horse pasture. " You work hard and you work well. A neighbour comes over to say hello. You ask her why she is visiting you." She laughed brittlely. " Is that a way to greet a neighbour, Carlin ? "

Matt found himself smiling. He was aware that the differences between these two girls were growing more pronounced each time he met them. Marjie was older, of course, but not much in years ; she was of a different character, more easy-going and quiet, and deep. This girl before him was like the wind ; and who can tell which way the wind will blow tomorrow ? Or today, for that matter ?

"Forgive an old bachelor," he said. "Yes, I'm plugging along, Miss Joyce. But of course, when I get a crew of men, it will go faster. How is your dad ? "

"Grumbling as usual. Lew Case told us you were down in Mexico—in Cristobal—looking for a crew. No luck ? "

Matt thought, Case told her I was in Cristobal. Maybe he was down there just looking around, as he said. Anyway, he isn't hiding his trip there ; guess I imagine too many things . . . " I'll get a crew, later. They'll come in any time now. Sometimes word goes slowly along the border towns."

" Gunmen ? "

"You have gunmen on your crew. Lew Case and Len

Ducom have ridden a few trails, and I don't think they were too straight. Down in Matador, the day I came to this country, your father and Lew Case were going to murder Dave Elwood."

She frowned. " I asked Father about that. He had been drinking a little too much, I guess, and then maybe Lew Case was over-anxious, too. For one, I'm glad you came along, Carlin." Her eyes were steady. " But you and Dad have nothing against each other."

" But it will come."

" Why ? Does it have to ? "

Matt was silent, building the thing in his mind. He realized she did not know about this other thing—these border men who rode that high mountain range, who ran guns through and who were not averse to stealing cattle too, and running them through. When they wanted Hank Davis' cattle they would take them when the moon was right, and Hank Davis would look at him with hard eyes. He thought he would tell her what he knew, and then he decided to keep it to himself. There was a time for each word, each action, each deed, and the present time did not seem appropriate.

" Let's hope I'm wrong. Won't you step inside what little bit of the cabin I've got finished and look it over ? "

He had the floor in place. He had hauled out sawed lumber from Matador, where an old man ran a small saw mill. " You'd better get the roof on before it rains," she said. " If it rains it will warp that floor." She ran a careful glance around, noting where the windows would be, where the partitions would come in, where the doors would fit. "It looks nice." She leaned back against the wall. "I'm tired, I guess. I better be going back home."

She went outside, that feeling of bafflement growing within her. She had come for one reason, and now she could not voice it because of her womanhood, and she had not been able to bring the conversation round to it because it had started out all wrong, because Marjie Elwood had been there and the thing had started wrong because of Marjie's presence.

She found her stirrup and went up. Matt Carlin laid his hand on the palomino's shoulder. "Thanks for coming over. I suppose, though, I'll be seeing you next Saturday night."

"Oh, Saturday night—why——" Then she understood. "Oh, you mean at the dance at Red Rock schoolhouse. Why, are you going?"

"Miss Marjie invited me to go. I suppose you'll be there?"

"Yes, I'll be there." One thing was settled anyway; she was glad now she had not put her thoughts into words, there in his cabin. That would have been humiliating, the more so because she had never asked a man to take her anywhere before. "I'll see you then. Good-bye."

When she reached the ridge a quarter of a mile to the north, the dusk was growing thicker, building in layers across the parched earth. The wind was moving aimlessly, drifting lazily through chamiso and ocotillo and manzanita, singing a little broken, simple song. The touch of it was cool; it lay across her cheeks, and she liked the cool fingers.

Joyce, she told herself, you'd better ride a strong saddle, girl. He doesn't give a damn whether you're alive or dead, he's so busy looking at Marjie Elwood. You'll hit a rough stretch if you don't watch out and you'll pile up your bronc and lose your saddle.... Ride easy, Joyce, and let things go smoothly for a while, and play your cards more skilfully. And if you don't have any luck in a few weeks, then discard the whole hand and let fate deal you a new bunch of cards....

You're acting crazy, another voice said.

When she forded Cottonwood Creek, a man rode out of the willows. Lew Case came up and said, "Damn it, girl, I wish you wouldn't ride across that stream. Matt Carlin's a hard man and from a distance he might mistake you for a man—a Bar Y rider. There's been more than one man shot from a distance with a rifle."

"I just rode in a ways looking for any of our stock that might have drifted across."

"Dangerous business."

"Damn you, Lew Case," she said angrily. "I don't need you for a bodyguard, nor do I need anybody else."

Case was silent.

They came to Piney Point and she saw a rider off to her left, going up Cottonwood Creek. Despite the distance she recognized him as the squat, beefy man she had seen on Circle W territory—the man who had been eating the sandwich.

"Who is that?" she asked.

Case looked. "A long way off," he said. "Maybe a Circle W hand—one of the Elwood men."

She glanced at him sharply, then looked away. She judged the distance the man was from her. She glanced back to where she had met Lew Case. The distance between them and that point was the same as the beefy man's distance from that same spot. Lew Case and the man had evidently met there in the willows. And when Case and she had ridden out, the stranger had hidden in the willows until they were out of sight. Now Case was denying recognition of the man.

She thought, Maybe I'm wrong.

Case said. "There's a dance at Red Rock school Saturday night. I'm a-wondering if you'll go with me, Miss Joyce."

She considered. "All right," she said.

NINE

The dusk was heavy when Marjie Elwood rode into the ranch. She left her horse at the barn and went to the big log house. The shadows were heavier inside. Dave Elwood sat at the table, a quart whiskey bottle in front of him, and Zeke Pandrill sat opposite him. The Mexican bandit lifted dark, unfathomable eyes and rose, bowing a little too low.

"Miss Marjie, so good to see you. Where have you been?"

The girl said angrily, "Ask one of your riders when he comes in at dark, Pandrill. He's trailed me all afternoon. Why don't you put a better man on my trail, one that is not so easy to see?"

Zeke Pandrill bowed again, more stiffly this time. "I am sure the *señorita* has made the meestake, *Señor* Dave. Perhaps one of our men has been out riding and looking over the co'ntry as you *Americanos* say, and Miss Marjie has made the meestake." She noticed his words were too smooth.

Dave Elwood asked, "What do you want?" and his voice was a little too harsh.

"Do I have to ask your permission to come into a house that I own half of?" she asked.

"I go," said Pandrill. "I see you again, Dave."

"Maybe," said Elwood.

The door closed behind the *bandido*. Marjie Elwood heard his boots cross the porch and step down on the gravel walk. Only then did she speak. And her voice was low and husky.

"What does he want you to do now?"

"What difference does it make to you?"

Her gaze was steady and without rancour. Rather her eyes showed a sort of defeat, a terrible tiredness. He saw this and felt a bit of remorse, but then he pulled this aside and let his front take over. He saw the weariness leave her eyes and saw something else come into them, and he had seen this change before, too.

"Poor misguided man," she said. "That's all you are, Dave. I've said it before and I guess I'll say it again some other time."

"And a hell of a lot of good it will do you!" Dave Elwood reached for the bottle. The rim of the bottle's neck rattled slightly against the glass tumbler as he poured a shot of the liquid into the vessel. "I guess when the devil made you woman he used the same mould and that mould had a sharp tongue, a bitter tongue. Now where, may I ask, did Miss Marjie Elwood, the great evangelist, spend the afternoon? With Matt Carlin, I suppose."

She nodded.

"You see him a lot," he said, as though reminiscing. "Too much, I guess. Maybe that's going to cut me and my darling sister a little apart, huh? Or, as Zeke would say it, no?"

She ran this through her mind. She felt of it, examined it, and found a clue there. "Then you and Zeke Pandrill intend to rustle Matt Carlin's cattle, is that it? You used to steal Davis' Bar Y stock, and now, since you sold your cattle, you intend to steal them back and sell them below the line?"

He shrugged. "You jump to conclusions. You will find they make a weak saddle string." He had let the conversation run the wrong way—this irked him. "You want a drink?"

"Something," she said, "anything. I have to wash this taste from my mouth." Zeke Pandrill had told Dave a little but he had not told him all. Pandrill was smart, he was pointed; he would let him in on a little and, because he could not leave the house very well, Pandrill would feed him a little money and run the same old game—the game she wondered, many times, if he did not realize. She walked to the kitchen and came back with a clean glass. She poured a stiff drink into it.

He said, "Lift your glass."

She did.

He said, " To the future," and drank. Still she held her glass. He looked at her sharply. " Why don't you drink ? "

" Not to the future, Dave."

He threw his glass on the floor. The gesture was typical of him—an adolescent, immature, melodramatic gesture. Shreds of tinkling glass slipped across the floor. She drank then, a smile tight across her lips.

He turned and left.

She went to the window. She could hear him moving ; he was in his room. She turned and looked at the table. He had taken the whiskey bottle with him. She closed her eyes and leaned back against the casing. The old *mozo* came in carrying a lamp. He put it on the table, lit it, and went out again, and once more the house was silent. She had her thoughts.

She should leave, she realized. Time and circumstances had run against her, and only God could help him. She could do nothing. She had tried ; she had used various means. When she had been considerate he had been cynical and cruel. When she had been domineering his cynicism had grown stronger. When she had become pleading he had become scornful. She saw no other method, so she became apparently indifferent. But deep down inside she knew, and she thought he knew, that she would never leave him as long as he drew breath into his wasted lungs.

She blew out the lamp and went into the night. As she entered her cabin, Zeke Pandrill came out of the shadows. He asked, " I'd like to see you—inside, *Señorita* Marjie."

She studied him momentarily. " All right."

He followed her in and she shut the door. He sat down on a chair while she cleaned the lamp chimney and touched a match to the wick. His silence was growing heavy on her and she tried not to notice it. When the lamp was burning properly she adjusted the wick to the right height.

" Well ? "

" Your brother he ees going to die sometime, no ? "

" We all are going to do that."

He regarded her with dark eyes. She saw that he was trying

to find a proper method of introducing his thoughts, of expressing the words he had come to say. She decided to get it over with.

"You didn't tell Dave that you had been stealing his cattle, I suppose, even before Matt Carlin came?"

"Why do you say that? I steal cattle——"

She interrupted. "I know what you and your men have been doing, Pandrill. I know that burro pack-train went through the other night and I know Dave was drunk and senseless in bed when you and your men took it through. I know you used to steal Circle W cattle and run them through Brush Canyon and Dave would never know it. You'd hand him some whiskey money and tell him the next day that they had been Davis' Bar Y stock. I got eyes and ears."

Zeke Pandrill leaned his head back against the wall. She stood and watched him. Finally his eyes swung back to her.

"Your brother, you do not tell heem thees? And why, *señorita?*"

"What good would it do?" she demanded. She held her emotions in sharp check. Anger was roiling through her. Anger not directed so much toward this insolent border bandit but rather toward Dave Elwood, the last of his male clan, and too ignorant to understand this simple Mexican *bandido*, this man of Yaqui and Irish and mixed bloods.

"What do you mean?"

"He is like his father," she said wearily. "He has a terrible temper. If I told him, he would get his guns and go against you and your men and you would kill him. Maybe you'd like me to do that, Pandrill. Maybe then you could get him out of the way."

"You talk mad—loco. You are like rest of women——"

He didn't say any more. Her open palm saw to that. When she stepped back the mark of her slap was plain across his swarthy face.

"Don't compare me with your border prostitutes," she said.

Anger ran across his dark eyes, fought there with discretion, and the common sense finally won. She had pulled back against the table and had opened the drawer. He saw the gun there. A Colt ·45, dark and blue against the light, and her hand was on it. He pulled himself back into his Latin shell. The Irish came through ; he smiled crookedly.

" You have jumped to conclusions, *señorita*." His voice had its old indifferent purr. " But now, for the first time, we know where we stand, no ? " His forehead pulled down into a scowl. " But thees man—thees Matt Carlin—you see heem and maybe you talk, and then he know."

She said, " He knows about you now."

" You misunderstand again. Thees Carlin, he does not know that we have been stealing Circle W cows, and he does not know now. He does not know that."

She considered, her hand still on the gun. " He'll find out sooner or later, I suppose. You knew him before, I understand. Is he an outlaw ? " He was silent for a moment, and she asked, " Does the law want him ? "

" No."

She felt a strange relief. She knew why, too, for the thing had been building up in her. She was a woman. She felt again a sagging of purpose, a sense of relief. There were two men now in her life, and in her hands lay their futures. No, that was not true, she thought, because Dave's future was what he and fate and his ideas made it.

She said, " I won't tell him."

He nodded. " I take your word." He took off his big hat and bowed. " The *señorita* will be in peace, always." He was smiling when he straightened, and she had the feeling suddenly that behind that smile was something lost, something gone, something of another day.

She was thinking of that when he went to the door and stepped out into the night. She had glimpsed beyond the man's exterior, she had seen in an unguarded moment something inside of him, and, strangely, it reminded her of what she had seen in her brother's eyes. The essence of it had been the same—the quality of it had told of loneliness, of the tiredness that only a man can know, the weariness that a woman cannot understand, and can never comprehend.

She bolted the door and blew out the lamp. She opened a

window and stood before it for a few moment, feeling the coldness of the outside air. She undressed slowly and pulled her nightgown on. She went to her bed and knelt and put her head upon the covers.

She did not pray aloud. She prayed silently.

TEN

Red rock schoolhouse was situated in the cottonwoods along a mountain creek. Beyond it stood the high butte of red clay that had given the school its name and farther along beyond that stood the dark bulk of the Sangre de Madres. When Matt Carlin and Marjie Elwood rode into the yard the dance was in full swing. Lamplight showed through the windows and the music of the violin and piano and accordion made a raucous medley.

They tied their horses in the trees. Marjie had ridden side-saddle and she wore a party dress that accentuated her blonde hair. Matt saw the scattered brands of the Matador country on the horses tied to the racks and the wheels of buggies and spring-wagons—Davis Bar Y horses, Heart Bar Nine broncs, some Circle W horses that Dave Elwood had kept and that some of his riders were using. There were other brands, too; these were evidently from the smaller outfits located west of Matador along the rim of the desert.

Matt asked, " Is Dave coming ? "

" No. He wasn't up to it, he said."

" There's Hank Davis' horse."

Marjie frowned. " Yes, and there's Lew Case's horse, and Len Ducom's. Most of Dave's riders came over—there is Mack Williams' bronc. Somebody told me Joyce Davis was coming with Lew Case."

" They go together ? "

" The first time that I know of," said Marjie.

Matt was frowning a little when they entered the kerosene-lighted room. There were all the ingredients of trouble there in the schoolhouse, and if somebody took to drinking that trouble might materialize—and travel damned fast. They stood in the doorway for a while and Marjie exchanged greetings with various women seated on the bench along the north side of the room.

"You'll want to meet some of the women, Matt," she said. She introduced him to them, going down the line—she knew them all regardless of age. Most of them were the wives of ranchers and small cowmen, and some were girls from Matador and neighbouring territory.

Matt was slightly bored, not particularly interested. He wasn't, at his best, much of a party man. The starting of the music somewhat saved his composure. Marjie danced well, her body lithe against him, and as they circled the hall he glanced at the other dancers.

Lew Case was dancing with Joyce Davis. Joyce said, "Why, hello, Mr. Carlin," and then to Marjie, "Hello, Marjie."

Case glanced around. "Howdy, Miss Elwood," he said. Then to Matt: "Hello, Carlin, want a drink?"

"No thanks."

Marjie murmured, "He's almost drunk now," and leaned her head against Matt's shoulder. Her hair was sweet and fresh in his nostrils and he felt a weariness enter her. "There might be trouble, Matt; maybe you shouldn't have come. Maybe we'd better go."

"We just got here," said Matt, smiling. "We can't leave now, Marjie."

The music died to a slow stop and Matt escorted her to the bench with the rest of the women. Hank Davis came up with a heavy-set young woman and bowed and thanked her for the dance. Then he straightened and looked at Matt, his eyes heavy under the craggy brows.

"And how are you, Mr. Carlin?"

"Fine," said Matt. "And you?"

"Fair to middlin', you might say. Would you step outside and have a drink with me, Carlin? A drink to the future of your Circle W spread." The stocky cowman swayed a little in his Justins. He was, Matt noticed, slightly drunk. His breath also told Matt that.

Matt smiled. "You got the wrong man, Davis, but thanks

just the same. You see, I never drink anything stronger than beer."

Davis said, " You mean you don't want to drink with me ? "

Matt hesitated momentarily. He would have to handle this with kid gloves ; the heavy-set cowman was drunk and touchy. " I'm sorry, but don't get me wrong. Of course I'd drink with you—if I drank. Thanks though."

" That's right," said Hank Davis, " I've heard that you never touch hard stuff." The music had started again and Lew Case danced by with a dark-haired girl. He swung the girl around and asked, " What's the trouble, Hank ? "

" Not a damned thing," growled Hank Davis. " If Matt Carlin doesn't care to drink with me it's none of your damned lookout, Case ! "

Case grinned. " You're gettin' tanked up, Hank," he murmured. He glanced at Matt and his eyes were sombre pools. " Maybe he's just too good to drink Matador whiskey, huh ? "

" Don't start anything here," snapped Davis.

Case danced away. Hank Davis said, " So long, Carlin," and went down the bench toward a rancher's wife. They danced into the crowd, and Matt turned, looking for Joyce Davis. He went to her. " This dance, please, Miss Joyce."

" I notice something odd," said Joyce slowly as they moved out on the floor. " I'm Miss Joyce but Marjie Elwood is just Marjie. Pray, sir, what is the difference between us ? You've known each of us about the same length of time, I believe."

Matt smiled. " All right, Joyce."

She was moving with him, blending into his movements, becoming a part of him. Her hair reflected facets of dancing lamplight and Matt felt some of the tenseness leave him. When supper time came Marjie and Matt ate sitting on the orchestra platform, watching the kids chase each other around the room. Marjie was a little too quiet and Matt knew why.

Many of the men were drinking, and so were a few of the women. Lew Case was getting pretty drunk and so was Len Ducom. Matt had seen Ducom and Case slip out of the room

F

a number of times, and once he had seen them go out with Mack Williams. Williams had a bottle in his hip pocket.

A tensity of feeling was building up until it was a tangible thing in the smoke-laden atmosphere, and Matt knew that it was directed against him. He was new to this range, and he had bought into it, and he was not welcome and he knew why.

" Maybe we'd better go," said Marjie.

" No man's driving me away until I want to go," said Matt.

After supper the festivities began again. This dance, Matt knew, would last until daylight. He had stepped out once during intermission for a breath of fresh air and a cigarette. Case and Ducom had been standing just outside the door and Matt caught the stale odour of whiskey on their breaths.

Ducom said, " Going home so soon, Carlin ? "

Matt turned and looked at him. " Why, no. Why ask ? "

Ducom was critically cold. Case moved to one side and Matt glanced at him—Case had his hand on his gun. Case was not puffing his cigarette now ; the Durham and wheat straw lay limp on his bottom lip, the coal dying. Beyond him and to Case's right stood Mack Williams, and Williams, too, had his hand on his holstered gun. Matt wondered at this gesture on Williams' part, and then dismissed it from his mind.

Ducom held the key. He could either reach or shrug the moment off. He did the latter ; the tension passed. " Just asked," he said.

Mat said, " I see."

He went over and leaned against a cottonwood tree, his back against the rough bark, and watched the men who came out of and entered the schoolhouse. The night air was cool and the wind was moving on the higher reaches. He ground his cigarette under his boot and let the freshness of the spaces move into him and possess him, and when the music started he went back into the hall.

He had the first dance with Marjie and the second with Joyce. There was a big, blocky man at the end of the hall, and

Joyce saw that Matt nodded to him. " Who is he ? " she asked.

" He's Hans Johnson," he said. " A cattle buyer." He didn't add that Johnson bought and sold wet cattle nor did he add that he wondered what Johnson was doing on Matador range. " Why do you ask ? "

" I've seen him somewhere before."

Matt glanced at her. Now where had she seen Hans Johnson ? Joyce, too, was wondering the same. Then her memory recalled the man she had seen the day she had ridden to Matt's place. The man who had sat beside the trail eating his lunch, and whom she had seen later when she met Lew Case and who she was sure had also met Case along the willows of Cottonwood Creek.

" I remember now," she told him.

Matt shrugged. " I see," he said.

The music ended with a blare and Matt escorted her to the bench. There was a slight commotion at the end of the hall by the door and he turned. Four men were standing there, dusty from the trail—four men who carried their guns tied down and who stood in a compact group.

Matt said, " Excuse me, Joyce," and went to one of the men, a short, wizened man of about forty who wore run-over boots and worn range trappings. He kept the emotion out of his voice as he said, " Damnit, Joe Hawkins, I never figured you'd get here. Been looking for you, fella."

Joe Hawkins' beady eyes twinkled. " Word reached us in Juarez, Matt. Damn, you look fine, man." Those eyes appraised Matt carefully. The bond between these two was a strong one. They had shared the same grub, ridden the same remuda, slept under the same sougans. What one had the other had and each knew that. " A coupla your old friends came with me."

Willy Day was an oldster, bald-headed and scraggly-whiskered, without a tooth in his head. Slim Kirkpatrick was a short man, not over five feet two, but he was deadly. Matt had seen him in action. Dippy Bullon was a kid, not more than twenty, but already the sun and long rides and powder smoke had set him apart. His boyishness was gone, lost before its time, and he would never regain it.

Hank Davis came up. " Your men, Carlin ? "

Matt said, " My crew, Davis."

" Gunslingers," said Davis. " Killers."

Joe Hawkins asked, " Who is this salty old walrus, Matt ? "

" Davis," said Matt. " He owns the Bar Y, a local outfit. He's drunk."

Hawkins' dark eyes hardened. " Shall I overlook the old gent ? "

" Best idea."

Davis moved ahead, then stopped. " This range is full of gunslingers, Carlin," he said to Matt. " And now, by hell, you're bringing in more ! " He was drunk, too drunk, and Matt shoved him back, shoved him hard. Davis almost fell down, but he recovered himself, his hand on his gun.

" No man's pushin' me——"

" I am," said Matt Carlin.

A man said, " No shooting here, please," and a woman screamed. Then the hall was silent save for the men who came toward them. The women sat on the benches, silent and still with fear. Joyce Davis came and took her father's arm.

" Dad, please, no trouble ! Dad listen—You're drunk ! "

Hank Davis tried to jerk free, but his daughter held his arm. Blustering rage coloured the cowman's beefy jowls. Matt turned slightly and looked at Lew Case, who stood to one side, his hand low. Len Ducom stood by the door and watched with small eyes.

Willy Day and Slim Kirkpatrick and Dippy Bullon were very silent, feeling the situation out, and sensing danger in it. They moved out a little, leaving a few feet between them, and they were ready for whatever came. Joe Hawkins stood there, his eyes missing nothing.

A hard hand jerked Matt around. Matt hit hard, hit without looking. His blow knocked Len Ducom against the wall. Ducom almost went down. The man stood alone against the wall, and then he twisted and went for his iron. But Matt had anticipated this, and he was settled, and he shot Ducom twice through the chest. The roar was loud in the hall. Ducom shot once and his bullet went straight down, missing his boots, ripping into the floor. Ducom fell.

Matt turned, and then Joe Hawkins had his weapon out. Dippy Bullon was right behind Joe, and Slim Kirkpatrick and Willy Day had their guns palmed. The roar had died, a woman screamed again. Hank Davis had stepped back, shocked and sober now, and Lew Case had his gun half drawn. Case looked at Matt's jutting Colt, then lifted his hand.

Case said, " You'll pay for this, Carlin."

" He had no right to lay his hands on me," said Matt. He was cold, deliberately cold, yet inside he was shaky. " He went for his iron first. I shot him in self-defence."

A man said, " He's right."

Women were going out the back door. The gun play had broken up the dance. Joyce Davis took her father's gun, took that of Lew Case. " Now go, Carlin," she said. Len Ducom's wheezing breath was loud in the room.

Matt nodded at his men. " Go," he said. They went out, and he looked at Hank Davis. " If you'da kept your big mouth shut this wouldn't have happened, Davis." He glanced at Len Ducom. " The doctor's here, ain't he ? "

" He's coming," said a man.

Matt said, " He'll probably live." But he knew otherwise. Ducom had been fast, his draw unexpected, and Matt had shot hurriedly. He had not had time to place his shots accurately.

He went outside.

Hawkins and Day and Kirkpatrick were already in the saddle and Bullon was going up. Their guns were rock-like in their fists. Matt stepped into leather and turned his horse. Marjie Elwood came running to him, holding her dress with one hand. She said, " Matt, oh, Matt ? "

" Here."

She put her hand on his horse's shoulder. She panted, " Matt, ride out, please. Case is wild, hog-wild. So is Hank Davis. Ducom died—just a moment ago. I'll ride home with one of our men. Please go, Matt."

Matt leaned low and kissed her. The impression was brief. Her lips were moist, and that was all. He lifted his head as Lew Case and Joyce Davis came into the light. Joyce had Case's gun and she had seen him kiss Marjie.

Her eyes were without emotion. Yet he had the impression suddenly that they hid a turmoil of thoughts that ran behind their veiled exterior.

ELEVEN

They took len ducom's body to Matador, tied across his saddle, and then Lew Case and Hank Davis rode for the Bar Y, with the blocky Davis deep between horn and cantle. The sun was rising over the peaks and sending shadows and light across the border land. Case was light in leather and scowling.

" He's hell with his iron, Hank."

" You mean Carlin ? "

" Who t'hell else would I mean ? " Case was quiet then, letting his thoughts branch out, letting them get form and strength. He knew now, more than ever before, that he would have to kill Matt Carlin. Although he and Ducom had been friends, nothing had really bound them together—their companionship had been based on necessity and not admiration. He mulled this thought over and knew that he would not kill Matt Carlin because Carlin had killed Ducom. He would kill Matt Carlin for only one reason : Matt Carlin stood in his way, and in the way of Humphries and Williams, and in the path of Zeke Pandrill.

" Tough man," murmured Hank Davis. He too, was silent ; he rolled his thoughts, and they tasted bitter. A little whiskey had got the best of him, and that thought hurt his stubborn pride. Carlin had killed one of his men—one of his riders—and that was, he thought, an insult against him, against his pride, against his Bar Y iron. Or was it ?

" Maybe not too tough, Hank."

Davis shifted in saddle. " Joyce is a goner," he said. " She's got a trap loaded for him, Case. Now why in the hell did all this have to happen to me ? You've seen her, ain't you, when she looked at him ? I watched them when they were dancing back there."

"Never noticed it, Hank. A woman is crazy. I've said it before and I suppose I will say it again."

"You hit the nail."

Again they were silent. Only the patter of their broncs' hoofs along the dusty trail and the creak of latigos and saddle trees. This, and their thoughts. Case ran over this new problem, viewed it from all angles, and tried to read a new menace in it.

He didn't care about Joyce Davis. She was a woman— a pretty woman—and she had some effect on him, some attraction, it was true. But that was as far as it went, and no further. A woman was a woman—he had had his share of them, and if another came and became too pressing—well, a man can't run all the time from them. . . . He wanted no part of Joyce Davis. He wanted a stack of American currency, and he would get this by working with Zeke Pandrill, just as would Humphries and Williams. And if he had not been killed, Len Ducom would have gotten the same. Maybe, for that matter, it was just as well that Ducom had been killed. One less piece of pie to be dished out—a piece he divided between himself and Humphries and Williams and Pandrill.

He thought, Maybe I can use Joyce, though, and then wondered where. He knew that one thing was paramount: there must always be strife between Hank Davis and Matt Carlin. They would have to be kept at pistol lengths or else both, or either, might divert too much attention to him and Pandrill and the others. The system was old and tried and had been worked many times. Get them fighting among themselves and then, while they were fighting, steal what they were fighting over when they were so deep in combat they were not watching their prize. . . . Divide them and conquer them. . . .

These thoughts were with him when they rode into the Bar Y corrals. They stripped their horses, tossed their saddles on the corral bar, and went into the cook shack. The Bar Y men, who had come directly across country from Red Rock, had already eaten and hit the hay in the bunkhouse and, save for the Yaqui cook, they had the long table to themselves.

Joyce entered and sat beside her father.

" When are they going to bury him, Dad ? "

Hank Davis chewed his mush and swallowed it. " Damn that injun," he said, " and his red hot grub ? Can't he never cook nothin' without heating it in the fires of hell ? We bury him Monday."

" Here on the ranch ? "

" In town."

" What did the coroner say ? "

Hank Davis looked at her roughly. " Hell, they ain't no case against Matt Carlin, woman. Len Ducom reached first and he didn't reach fast enough. He started the ruckus and danged near everybody on Matador range saw it. We can't get no warrant out for Carlin."

" He's a killer," said Case.

" You drove him into it," said the girl angrily. " You were drunk, the whole bunch of you, and you were looking for trouble ! "

" Whoa up," said Hank Davis, " whoa up, Joyce." He was quiet now, strangely quiet, and she sensed something significant in this. It was not long in coming. " You've gone pretty much for him, haven't you ? "

Her eyes were without thoughts. Finally she gave in. " Is it that apparent, Dad ? "

Hank Davis said, " Watch yourself, daughter, and don't lose your head, honey. He's seen guns and he's seen women." The gruffness had left him and he was speaking softly, as a father speaks to an errant child. " Don't let yourself go too far, because there might be something in you that wouldn't be the same afterwards and that might hurt you the rest of your life. You can't die of a broken heart, as the poets and song writers say you can, but it can raise hell with your life for a long, long time. And I know—I married your mother, raised you, and your mother passed on. But I'm talking like a man shouldn't talk, I guess."

Case said, " Excuse me, please," and got to his feet and went outside. Joyce laid her head on her father's shoulder. It was the gesture of a child, a small child, and it touched him. Case saw this, from the doorway.

Case walked out into the brilliant morning sun. His spur rowels made a soft sound against the harsh squeak of the slowly turning windmill. He went to the horse corral and roped a bay stud and saddled him. The stud was full of energy; he arched his stallion neck and fought the bit. Case smiled and went up and spun him, running the fight out of him.

He turned the stud toward the Heart Bar Nine. He let the animal lope until a fine thick lather grew around the edges of the Navaho saddle blanket and foam flecked from the spade bit and split-ear headstall. The edge left the cayuse and Case let him fall to a trot, then to a walk.

Nobody was in the house, of course, and he found himself looking absent-mindedly for Len Ducom; then memory brought back the fact that Ducom was dead. A gallon jug rested under the table and he lifted it. There was a note under it, and he read it with cold indifference and then threw it into the stove and set it on fire. He went to a room and rolled into the dirty, unmade bed and slept until the night was heavy.

He got up, lit the lamp, and fried some eggs and bacon and made some black coffee. He was eating when a low voice called from the back door, " Who's inside ? "

" Me, Case."

" Pull down the blinds," said the voice. " I'm coming in."

Case pulled down the shades. " Come in, Humphries," he said.

Jack Humphries came inside. He said, " We can't let anybody see us together; that's why I asked you to pull down the shades before I come in. Place looks sort of vacant without Len around."

" Where's Mack Williams ? "

" He'll come along directly, I reckon. He never went to the *hacienda* after the dance; he bedded down on Spring Crick line camp."

" They get the cattle through all right last night ? "

Humphries shrugged. " Guess so, Lew. Zeke Pandrill rode into the ranch right after noon today and hit the blankets. Came in alone. Said his men had decided to stay a day or two in Cristobal." He stopped and listened to something outside. " Men by the door."

" Come in," said Case.

The door opened and Mack Williams and Zeke Pandrill entered. Williams said, " I met this old greaser coming this way, so we rode in together." Pandrill nodded and smiled, showing his teeth.

Case asked, " Did the herd get through last night ? "

Pandrill said, " *Si*, we got it through. They are in a canyon beyond Cristobal. Hans Johnson was not there to pay for them, so the men held them. I heard Johnson was at the dance ? "

" Damned if I know why the fool was there," growled Case. " He knew we were stealing Circle W cattle last night—stealing them while Matt Carlin was at the shindig. This Carlin is a tough man, Zeke. He killed Len Ducom and never batted an eye. But I guess Johnson must've hit back across the border, because he left a note under the whiskey jug telling me he had eaten here and then ridden for Cristobal." He glanced sharply at Zeke Pandrill. " Who'll get the money for that stolen beef if you aren't there to collect it from Johnson ? "

" Pedro Gonzales."

Case's eyes tightened. " I wonder about him—sometimes," he said. He saw the dangerous look in Zeke Pandrill's black eyes and he changed the subject. " Carlin's got a crew, a gun-crew, and they ride with quick guns."

" I know them," said Pandrill.

Case leaned back in his chair. He glanced at Humphries, then at Williams, and then looked at Zeke Pandrill. This whole thing, the whole set-up, was pulling in tighter and time was building the stage and time would bring about the climax. He leaned back and said, " How many head of cattle can Johnson take ? "

" All we can send him," said Pandrill.

Williams spoke. "There's about six hundred Circle W cows grazing around Warner Springs, Zeke. Just right to be bunched and shoved through Brush Canyon. Me and Humphries saw them there the other day. Pretty fat stock, too. How about them in a few nights?"

"Might," said Pandrill, "and we might not. Next week I got a shipment of guns coming through." The renegade was quiet, too quiet. "I've seen a few riders, off in the distance, the last couple of days, and they got me to thinking."

"Rangers?" asked Case.

Pandrill lifted lazy eyes. "Could be," he said. "Might be. I'll run some of my men on circle and see what they pick up. What's your idea of affairs between Davis and Carlin, Case?"

"Davis crossed him at Red Rock, Pandrill. Carlin ain't so set for Davis—he can see Hank Davis is an ornery old bull—but I got a hunch that Davis is ready for Carlin. They had a sort of set-to, right before Len Ducom pulled against Carlin."

"Humphries told me about that."

Williams asked, "Well, what's next?"

Silence moved across the room and held them for some time. Case was rocking a little on his chair, sitting on the two hind legs only, and his eyes seemed lazy, yet they were deceptive. Humphries had pulled down into his shell—he was thin as he hunkered beside the wall, rolling a cigarette with slow fingers. Williams was the same—a slouchy, unkempt man without much hope or motivation, who had seen what was coming and had not bothered to step aside, taking it as only a part of the days allotted to him to breathe air and feel the rain and sunshine.

Pandrill said, "Brand a couple of Circle W calves with the Davis Bar Y iron. But don't take small, suckling calves—get some unbranded yearling stock. They won't make it look too set-up and staged, huh? Carlin knows that Davis would never be fool enough to run his iron on one of the Circle W suckling calves. So pick out one that has stopped sucking its cow."

Case put his chair on its four legs. " That'll be a good idea, Zeke. When Carlin sees the Calves he'll ride over to the Bar Y and accuse Hank Davis of stealing his stock."

Pandrill held up a dark, chubby hand for silence. " But first, in a night or two, we take these cattle, these six hundred or so, and we chouse them into Mexico, and Johnson buys them." His eyes were sharp and bright on them. " Then we brand these calves, huh ? "

Humphries and Williams nodded. Case said, " All right, Zeke. But when do us three get our cut from this last herd, the one you took through last night ? "

" When Johnson buys the cows."

Case was silent. Then, " All right."

" You theenk I would not pay, huh ? "

Case shrugged. " Just a statement, Zeke, no more, no less." He stretched, yawned. " Me, I'm goin' to hit the hay." He went into his bedroom. He put his gun under his pillow and left the door blocked and the blind down and he lay there in the silent dark. After a while he heard horses moving across the distance, and he knew then that Pandrill and Williams and Humphries were riding back to the Elwood *hacienda*, and that made him think of Dave Elwood. . . .

Dave was lying in bed, too, probably, and Dave, too, was looking into the dark, was feeling the night's coolness and its stillness. There was this difference between them : Case would see the sunrise of many days, and that thought did not bother him, but Dave Elwood had but few sunrises left. Lew wondered if Elwood thought of that.

And he wondered why he was thinking of Dave Elwood. . .

TWELVE

After the arrival of Joe Hawkins, Willy Day, Slim Kirkpatrick and Dippy Bullon, the building programme spurted on Tumbling creek. Matt Carlin had suddenly acquired the strength and industry of eight more hands and the cabin went up rapidly. The barn, also made of logs, came into sight, too.

Matt had acquired the semblance of an outfit. He had two wagons, three sets of harnesses, three work teams, plenty of saddle horses; and trips to Matador had furnished axes, grub, and the dozens of other essentials necessary to the continued operation of a cow outfit. They even had a forge and a workshop and plenty of horseshoes and an anvil.

"What about these cows?" asked Joe Hawkins. "We oughta round up these dogies and run your iron on them, Matt. You got a wad of money walkin' those hills and buttes and that walkin' dinero ain't packin your iron or anybody else's iron, for that matter. That unbranded stuff, according to the laws of the range, belongs to the man who runs his hot iron on them."

"We have to build this place up first," said Matt. "Then we'll use this as a point of operations. If you've taken time to notice, I've set this house just about in the middle of my range. From here to any point on my grass is about the same distance. This is the centre of the hub. That will make it easier to work a wagon out in the rough country, and we can hold some along the creek too."

Hawkins scowled, shifted his cud and spat. "I know that, Matt. But this morning, when I rode to the Circle W for the brandin' irons, who do you figure I saw over there but Zeke Pandrill? And when Pandrill's in the country and there's an unbranded cow—or a branded cow—around loose, that cow goes with Pandrill. He seems to have a mournful attraction for a cow, and they follow him just like a magnet, so he claims. But me, I always figure he wasn't in the lead, and I still maintain that the cow was ahead of him with him chasin' her. Sure, you say he's runnin' guns—well, that's true. But he might be mixing in a few cows with those guns, too. That Mex revolution army of Pancho Gomez's is just like any army—it marches on its stomach, like Napoleon or some big-wig said years ago."

"Zeke Pandrill cross my path," said Matt, "and I'm killing him."

Joe Hawkins shook his head sourly. "He's a right smart mix-up of a lot of blood, and he's got a sharp spot over his ears and he'll take a lot of killing, Matt."

"You don't like him, do you?"

"We've met before," said Joe Hawkins. "I sent a bullet through his guts and I still say I should have pulled my sights up and pushed it through his black heart. Zeke Pandrill never forgets or forgives. I'm ridin' high in my saddle and I've got eyes in the back of my skull."

"Ambush?"

"You're damned right."

Matt was quiet. "Maybe you shouldn't've come, Joe," he finally said. "I never knew things were that bad between you and Pandrill. I'd sort of feel responsible if anything did happen to you on his account."

"Be hell if I got killed," said Joe Hawkins. "One thing is, I sure wouldn't want to go to heaven and float around with a big nightgown on—*Dios*, that would be a picture, huh?"

Matt smiled. "You're a damned fool." They went into the corral where they saddled horses. Willie Day was working on the barn, and Matt pulled in. "Riding over the hills to see where we'll find the most beef on round up, Willie. Be back around sundown, I figure."

"Don't get lost," said Willie.

Almost a week had passed since the death of Len Ducom, and Matt had lost some of his tightness. The sun was warm, but not hot; they rode at a slow pace, enjoying the hills, the wind, the high-tipped peaks. Cattle were lazy along creeks and around water holes, browsing in the shade of box-elders and cottonwoods, but as they rode on the higher reaches the cattle were wilder. The animals saw them and turned and wheeled into the brush, running cleanly and fast and rippling the *chamiso* behind them as they disappeared.

" Two riders," murmured Matt.

Joe Hawkins moved his horse about twenty feet to one side. They were on a small mesa, and the two riders loped up, with the lead man lifting his hand high in the Indian sign of peace.

" Harry Perkins in the front," murmured Matt. " Do you know the other fellow, Joe ? "

" California Ed Dann, I think."

Matt shrugged. " Don't know him."

" California man," said Joe Hawkins. " Used to be marshal down at Chula Vista and National City when things were rough down that way. Boomed a lot and was with the Texas Rangers for a spell. A tough man but a just man. His word is like Harry Perkins', good."

" They got anything against you in this section ? " asked Matt quickly.

Joe Hawkins shook his head.

The pair rode up and split apart and pulled in. Perkins was a big man and his way of living had marked him. He had a hawkish nose and a hard mouth. California Ed was quick in his saddle, a thin man of fast movements. They exchanged greetings, and Perkins' smile was deceptive.

" Heard you had bought in this country, Matt. Glad to hear you're settling down. But it looks to me like you bought in on a corner of hell."

Matt nodded. " Looks like it, Perkins." He was biding his time, wondering just what these men wanted; he had a hunch why they rode this range. " My foreman, Joe Hawkins. You've met him, Perkins." He lifted his eyes to California Ed Dann, held his gaze. " You met Joe before, too, I take it, California."

"Yes," said California Ed. "But how did you know me?"

"Joe just told me."

Harry Perkins shifted in leather and said, "We're rangers, Matt. Arizona rangers. Don't jump to conclusions too hasty, fellow."

"I'm not," said Matt. "If I did, I'd have a gun in my hand. I've had a few kinks in my back-trail, but there ain't none there that an Arizona ranger'd be worried about, and I think the same thing holds true for Joe here and for my men at the ranch. Am I right?"

"Right," said Perkins.

"Then what's the deal?" asked Matt. "You aren't over here in the Sangre de Madres for your saddle boils, Perkins. Put your cards out and let me look at them."

Perkins glanced at California Ed, who was loafing listlessly in his saddle. He pushed his Stetson back and rubbed his sweaty forehead, Matt looked at the red ring his hat's sweatband had made around the lawman's heavy head. He was quiet inside. He already knew what Perkins would say, and he waited patiently.

"We're bucking the men and the guns you are bucking, Matt," said Harry Perkins. "There's a revolution in central Mexico—something you already know—but maybe you don't know somebody's smuggling guns across the border from around in this section."

Matt shrugged.

"We've been in the country for a month, working under cover. The whole set-up is becoming pretty clear now, and we should hit in a week or two. Zeke Pandrill's on this Sangre de Madre range, and where Pandrill is there is thievery and trouble. You've seen him, I reckon?"

Matt was thinking of Marjie Elwood. Dave was in this deep and soon he would have to pay, and that would hurt Marjie. And besides, more than one lawman had made his life miserable, back there in the days gone by, and he decided suddenly he'd play his own hand out.

"I don't know a damn' thing, Perkins." He said it bluntly.

G

"You tote a star and you draw pay from the territory. I've only been crossed once on this range. I killed the man who crossed me. I'm playing a clean hand; I'm not looking for trouble. When trouble comes to me I'll meet it with my guns or my fists or what little brains I got, but I'll wait for that time. I'm settled here, and a man can't stay when his back-trail gets trouble on it."

Harry Perkins said, "All right, Matt, well said. But the whole thing simmers down to this: we both got the same opposition. Maybe later. . . . ?"

"Maybe," said Matt.

Perkins considered that lightly. He had ridden this trail before and he knew the bends, the twists. The formula was old, but sometimes the pattern varied and took on new colours, and this added taste and spice to his life. He had gathered his philosophy out of trail dust and gunsmoke and human failings, and he knew that things would always end the same, regardless of what happened.

"Forget you saw us, Matt," he said. He turned his horse and rode off, with California Ed Dann loping beside him. They pushed across the mesa and the dip hid them until later they came out of the brush, riding towards Matador. Distance and the shimmer of the sun came in and claimed them and hid them.

"Well," said Joe Hawkins, "that's that—for the time being."

"Trouble ahead," murmured Matt.

Joe Hawkins' thin shoulders lifted. "One damned thing after another. That's what the drunk with the d.t.'s said when he thought he saw two devils chasing each other. *Quien Sabe, amigo?* Maybe they've taken the load off our shoulders regarding Pandrill and his riders. But there's still Hank Davis. Not that the old devil is much 'count —but Lew Case rides close to his gun."

Matt grunted, "Smoke always rises—sooner or later."

"Let's hope it's soon," said Joe Hawkins.

Late afternoon found them on the hill overlooking Warner's Springs. The long, slow ride had seeped into Matt, leaving a contentment in him. The wind had died and the dust behind their hoofs hung listlessly against the blue air. A week ago, he thought, Len Ducom had been breathing this air, his eyes had been on yonder mountains; and now they had weighted him down with sod in a dark, deep grave. The riddle was endless and ageless; it had no meaning or theme. The mystery of it was too great, too big in scope, for man ever to fathom it. Joe Hawkin's voice broke into his thoughts.

"Ain't many head of cattle down in that section, Matt, and when I was here about four days ago, there was quite a big herd grazin' down there." He took his gaze and ran it across the hills beyond the springs and held it there for some time. "They might have drifted off over yonder direction and hid themselves in those draws."

They rode down the slope, their horses sliding in shale and loose gravel. They came to the bottom of the coulee. A few head of cattle were bedded down in the buckrush, and they ran out when they saw the two riders. Manure on the ground showed that, a few days before, there had been quite a few head around the small creek made by the spring.

They rode south. But evidently a thunderstorm had swept across the region a few days before, and, when they got on a ridge, the tracks ran out where the water had washed them. Matt pulled in his horse. "Probably drifted up this way and ran into this local storm and drifted with it to the north. The heat down in the valley causes lots of thunderstorms."

"Rising air. Warm air. It rises fast and gets turbulent and the friction causes static electricity. The result is a hell of a commotion."

Matt glanced at him. "Where did you get all that knowledge?"

"Read it in a book once. Down in San Clemente in Jalisco province. Had to hole up there for a spell until a leg got okay. That damn' gent never had no manners at all. He just upped with that rifle and shot me through the ham. So I went to bed and read some Mexican *libros*." He squinted through the gathering dusk. "Let's ride to the north and look things over before it gets dark. This will be a hard place to run a round-up in. Steep land and wild cattle."

"We'll put the wagon down on the flat and run out circle riders. We'll work the cattle to the north and hold them along the bottom land. The cows must've drifted out of this country in front of that storm."

"Them Mexicans need a lot of beef, Matt. Them peons walk all the way, and they carry grub and ca'tridges with them and tote them heavy rifles. This beef would make good chewing across the line. Ever think of that?"

"Lots of times. . . . But so far I ain't seen no sign pointing toward the fact that Zeke Pandrill is rustling Circle W beef. Maybe he is. Maybe he ain't. But until I know for sure, I ain't got nothing to run on, Joe."

"He leaves a wiggly track," said Joe Hawkins.

They swung their mounts, heading for Tumbling Creek. When they reached Antelope Forks—where Tumbling and Spring Creeks converged—Dave Elwood came loping over the hill on a palomino. He saw them and swung his horse in their direction. They drew rein and waited.

Elwood's face was flushed. Matt found himself wondering whether it was his exertion or his physical condition that caused the man's colour. He introduced Joe Hawkins.

"Met Dave the other day," said Joe. "I was riding the south range and we met there. Seems like you get around a lot, Elwood."

"When I can," said Elwood. His glance was coldly indifferent. "Maybe I have a reason for riding, Hawkins."

Dave Elwood's tone was a little too gruff. Joe Hawkins squinted at him and then glanced off across space. Matt Carlin had the same impression again: this man was reckless and without a future because soon he would be dead. This fact was grating on him, despite his efforts to show the world otherwise, and each breath was a conscious reminder of that fact.

"Miss Marjie," asked Matt, "how is she?"

Elwood smiled. "She is well in physical health, of course,

but I guess it's hard on her to see me in this punk shape."
His eyes were bright and sharp with the fever that consumed him. " You have been some time away from the Elwood *hacienda*, Matt."

" Busy."

" Not because of Marjie ? "

Matt spread his fingers across the wide horn of his saddle. He regarded them with a studied silence. " A man is only a man, Elwood, and sometimes he rides the wrong trails. . . . I was hoping Marjie didn't feel that way about me, but I guess she does. I had hopes that maybe, after this all was cleared up—Well, a man can have his hopes, too."

Elwood said, almost bitterly, " Maybe I figure in on that, too, Carlin. Maybe you know why she lives her life so close ? "

" You're her brother, Dave," said Matt simply. " She's faithful and she's showing it. Maybe you're thinking wrong, fellow."

" Forget it," murmured Dave Elwood. The harshness had run out of him and left him almost boyish. " I don't think this thing will drag out too long, Carlin. Day by day I'm learning more and more, and that means I can't let it travel on at this pace. Maybe you know what I'm driving at ? "

Matt wondered, held his tongue. Had Dave Elwood discovered the real dirtiness, the real filth, in Zeke Pandrill's makeup ? Matt was on the point of asking the consumptive, then let the thought die unvoiced.

" I don't know a thing," he said.

Dave Elwood's eyes were heavy with his thoughts. Matt caught the sudden odour of stale whiskey on the man's breath. "Maybe it pays a man to be ignorant, Carlin." He turned his palomino. " *Vaya con Dios*."

" An odd man," murmured Joe Hawkins.

" Death," said Matt. " Death riding a saddle. Sometimes I think he's no good, that he's weak, and then again he seems strong, ruthless. That's funny, isn't it, that I can think that way about him ? Really, I should hate his guts —he sold me this spread and never told me what I was walking into. But, by God, I can't do it, Joe. Maybe it's pity because he's sick. Maybe it's because of his sister. She's a faithful woman and he knows it and her family ties are strong."

"She care for you?"

"I hope not. She's a good woman——"

"Good women get married," said Joe Hawkins. "Even some of the bad ones do. Me, I almost hooked up with a floozy in a bar in Juarez onct. But that's neither here not there. He's a funny gent, no two ways about that."

Matt turned in the saddle and glanced back at the Sangre de Madres. He could dimly see Dave Elwood riding south, riding into the dusk and the foothills. Later, when he looked, he could see him no longer.

Encroaching darkness hid him.

THIRTEEN

Dave elwood rode into the *hacienda* when the darkness was just getting its thickest. He had ridden slowly, letting the palomino set his own pace. The rim of the moon was colouring the Sangre de Madres when he stepped down and handed the reins to the old *mozo*.

"Tired tonight."

The old man showed regard. "You shouldn't ride so damn far, Dave."

Dave went to the house. He lit a kerosene lamp, took a drink from the quart bottle and sat down, a great unrest in him. He was sitting there looking idly at the door when Zeke Pandrill entered.

"Where you been, Dave?"

Elwood looked at him. "What the hell difference does it make to you?"

"You're drunk."

"One drink," said Elwood. "Just one." He got to his feet. "You got something to talk over with me, Zeke?"

"Nothin' in particular."

"I'm tired, damned tired. So why don't you go down to the bunkhouse and talk to the boys down there, Zeke?"

"Sorry." Zeke Pandrill got to his feet. His suave face showed anger; then he wiped it away. "Hope you feel better in the morning, Dave." He turned and went, his spur rowels clanging. They were made of Mexican *pesos* and they had the sweet musical sound of silver. Dave Elwood took another drink.

He went out in the hall and called, "Marjie," but he got no answer except from the echoes. Sometimes she slept in the house, and he went to her room. Before it had been his mother's room, and even yet it seemed to hold the scent of her presence, and he seemed to feel her personality. Then he went to the cabin and knocked on the door, even though the building was without lights.

" Who's there ? "

" Dave."

The bolt slid back and the door opened. She was a shadow against the darker shadows in the background. He went inside. " Don't you have a lamp ? "

" I didn't light it," she said. " I like to sit in the dark sometimes. It's there on the table. You may light it if you care to."

He stroked the match to flame against his chaps and the flickering light danced on the walls and across the floor. The wick caught, spluttered, and grew. He put the chimney on the lamp and looked at Marjie.

" How goes things, sis ? "

She studied him, her eyes critical. " Are you drunk again ? "

That hurt him, but he hid it. " Can't a man speak to his only sister ? " he said gruffly. " You say that my tongue is sharp, but sometimes I think——"

She was sorry. " I never meant to talk sharply, Dave," she assured him. " I guess maybe my nerves are a little upset, too. Where have you been all afternoon and this evening ? "

" Out on the range. Riding."

" Why ? "

He spread his thin fingers in an empty gesture.

" Ain't that just like a woman ? " he demanded of the walls. " When you're home they want you to ride out and when you do ride they want to know why you didn't stay home." His smile was tight across his thin lips. " I saw Matt Carlin and Joe Hawkins about dusk around Warner Springs."

" When are they pulling their round-up wagon out ? "

" Soon, I guess." He got to his feet and walked, for restlessness pushed him with stern hands. " Sometimes I guess I played Matt Carlin a dirty trick, Marjie. I got him to buy the Circle W, and maybe I didn't represent the spread for what it was."

She felt a hand tighten in her breast. " What do you mean by that, Dave ? "

He turned on her sharply, his voice a little shrill. " Do you think I'm ignorant ? Do you think I'm blind ? Don't you think I can hear, or see ? Zeke Pandrill's on this range. You know what that means, don't you ? "

" He and his men run guns into Mexico. You know that and so do I."

" What more do you know ? "

" Why, nothing, I guess."

" Rangers are moving in on Matador range, Marjie. Today I saw two strangers, and if they weren't rangers I'll eat your hat without salt. The net is pulling tighter and there'll be gunfire. If it gets into court that means it'll implicate me. And that'll drag you into the mess."

She was silent.

" Do you hear me ? " he demanded.

" I heard you."

He stopped, looked at her. Then the impact of the whole situation hit him and registered, and he knew his path from there on. Suddenly it lay clear and bright before him, and he could see the bends in it and the straight sections—it lay like a clean ribbon of hard trail that slid away and became lost under the harsh bright sun. And along that rail a man would walk alone.

" Matt Carlin likes you, Marjie."

" He's a fine man."

" He——" He stopped again, and again he felt the futility of trying to talk to her. There were walls between them, and though they were brother and sister, these walls came from their personalities and could not be surmounted. " Yes, he's a fine man," he repeated after her. " Good night, Marjie."

He went outside and closed the door behind him. He shut it slowly and carefully and walked toward the house. He stopped on the long porch and looked out over the ranch, looked at the lights in the bunkhouse and the cook shack. Horses were stirring in the corral and the fine silt of corral dust came from their hoofs. He thought of the bottle inside the house and then he thought of that night and the ride ahead. That ride would take a cold strength, not a strength motivated by whiskey. He went to the barn.

The old *mozo* was not around. He saddled a heavy black gelding and led him out the back way and circled the buildings and tied the horse in the buckbrush behind the house. He went inside and got a .30-.30 rifle and his whiskey bottle. He checked the rifle for loads. The brass cartridges were dull under the lamplight. He put the whiskey bottle in his saddle pocket and stuck the rifle into the saddle scabbard. He went to the bunkhouse.

Some of the hands were already in their bunks. A few others were playing poker around a table. Piles of pesos and American dollars were in the pot and in the stakes before each player. A couple of the players were Mexicans and the others were a mixture of half-breeds and Americans. He did not know all of them, for some were Zeke Pandrill's own hands and had come out of the border land and the deserts to Pandrill's side. They were a close clan: close-mouthed, close-eyed. They saw everything and said nothing about what they saw.

He saw that Jack Humphries was lying on his bunk. But he noticed that Humphries was fully dressed, even wearing his spurs. He dozed on his back with an old newspaper over his face to cut out the light. Dave Elwood stood there and watched the game for a while. Nobody spoke to him and he felt a slow resentment rising inside of him as he realized that this ranch, like himself, had slipped a long, long way.

He went to the cook shack. By Hell had a pot of hot coffee on the big range. He poured a cup of it and stirred in some sugar. The Oriental stuck his scraggly head through the door leading to his quarters.

"By Hell wonderin' who was out here, by hell. Glad to see you, Missy Dave. How goes the lungs?"

Dave nodded. "Better."

The Oriental's face showed a wide smile. "Glolly, all the time you tell By Hell that, and even if he knows you're lying, he still likes it, by hell. You want something else, Missy Dave? Clookie, clake, sandwich? I fix him for you."

"Just coffee. *Gracias*."

"I go to bed then. Daylight he come early, by hell. I think first you talk to this Pandrill. He comes in here late after cloffee and wakes me up. Sometimes I cut his throat with a butcher knife. My dull one, by hell. Watch him bleed. Glood night, Dave."

"'Night, By Hell."

The Chinese went back into the dark recesses of his room. The coffee was hot—not too hot—and Dave Elwood nursed the cup thoughtfully, filling it a number of times. Something inside of him called thirstily for whiskey, but he managed to throttle the inner man's voice by paying no attention to the urgent demand. He sat there about an hour, then went to the bunkhouse.

He did not go inside. He stood on tiptoe and looked in the high window. The poker players were still at it. He glanced at Humphries' bunk, but Humphries was not in it. Mack Williams was under the blankets in his bed and seemingly asleep. Dave Elwood went back to the barn.

Humphries' horse was gone.

He leaned against the barn, the moonlight spilling around him. He went to the *hacienda*, went in the front door and right out of the back to his horse. The animal nudged him as he mounted. He rode to the west, swinging wide around the cut-coulees and brush, riding the ridges and side-hills. He rode fast, standing on his stirrups, the rifle bouncing in the scabbard under his left stirrup.

He was making the first move, he was cutting himself from his ties, and he felt a push of contentment, a lift of his spirits. He started coughing and buried his mouth against his sleeve, waiting for the bitter spasm to pass. Finally it left him and he had thoughts only for the task ahead.

When he reached a high ridge, he pulled the black behind sandstones, and the tumbling, disorderly runs and dips of Matador range lay below him. His eyes picked out a trail and followed it and he saw the rider along it, a rider that pushed through the moonlight toward the north. His eyes, trained to distance, recognised the man as Jack Humphries, and he knew he was on the right track.

Accordingly he lifted the black with his rowels, sending the beast down the slope, working at a great tangent that would eventually take him to the Heart Bar Nine ranch house, a dark spot wrapped in somnolent shadows there on the mesa miles to the north. He had the hunch that other men were riding the range, for logic told him this would be true. Therefore vigilance rode at his elbow.

He came at last to the trail that Humphries had followed. He was, he figured, a mile south of the Heart Bar Nine. He took the black into the high *chamiso* and tied him and took the rifle from the scabbard. The steel of it was hot from the day's sun, despite the cold chill creeping across the high rangelands. He settled on his haunches, watching the trail, and when he had to cough he did so silently, burying his mouth against his sleeve.

Time ran out and the moon heeled over. He felt the sharp edge of impatience and remembered the whiskey bottle on his saddle. The thirst was dry against his palate, it ran on and became bitter; he fought against it. The fight was sharp for habit was deep. But he ran his strength against it and it went into the background.

The chill nipped him and he shifted position, still keeping the rifle ready. He wondered what time it was, and glanced at the moon. It had moved impersonally across space, and stratus clouds were leafy across its pocked surface. He judged that two hours had passed.

He heard approaching hoofs.

One horse, he thought. Hope it is Jack Humphries. And when the rider rounded the far bend he saw he had been correct: Humphries sat in the saddle. He watched the man approach and then he looked at the moon again. He thought, For centuries—for trillions of years—the moon has looked down and seen wars and death, hate and love. . . . Then he stepped out with his rifle under his arm.

He said, " Howdy, Humphries."

Ten feet away, Humphries had halted. Surprise was scrawled deeply across his loose face by the bitter pen of surprise. He reached out, gathered his composure, and his shoe-button eyes became without thought, without emotion.

" What the hell you doing here, Dave ? "

" I could ask you the same ! "

" Riding," said Jack Humphries.

" How's things at the Heart Bar Nine ? What plan did you and Zeke Pandrill and Lew Case cook up tonight to turn Matt Carlin and his men more against the Davis Bar Y, against old Hank Davis ? Hell, I know the whole sordid story, Humphries. You thought you were double-crossing me and I didn't know it. Pandrill thinks the same. So does Mack Williams."

" You're drunk," Humphries accused him.

" Right there," said Dave Elwood, " you lie ! "

Humphries lifted his thin shoulders. Seemingly the gesture was a shrug, but Humphries used it to catch Dave Elwood in him, and then Dave Elwood's bullets hit him and broke of guard. He brought his ·45 out of holster, his blood hot him and dumped him to the ground.

Dave Elwood stood there on one knee for some time, listening to the sounds die in the distance, listening to the anxious pawing of Humphries' horse that had wheeled and galloped away, then stopped when he got a rein snagged around his foreleg. Then he got to his feet and walked to the man who lay on his face in the dusty trail. He bent and turned him over and felt of his wrist. He held the wrist for some time, then let it drop lifelessly.

Dead, he thought.

He went to his horse. He put the rifle back and took the bottle from the saddlebag and drank deeply and then looked at the moon. It was the same—even the same clouds were in front of it—and the pocked yellow surface looked down on him with no emotion. He drank again, feeling the whiskey come into him and warming him. He found his stirrup and rose.

Two hours later he rode into the Elwood *hacienda*. The

once-proud *rancho* was without lights and huddled miserably under the moonlight. He unsaddled his black and turned him into the horse pasture.

The first one is dead, he told himself.

The black drank at the trough and then rolled in the dust. He turned and went into the house by the back door. the place was dark, of course. Some of the heat of day was still with it, and this felt warm and good. He had another bottle under his bed and he drank of that as he undressed. Then he lay in bed, his body under the blankets, and finally he sank into a drunken, dead sleep.

FOURTEEN

HANK DAVIS RODE INTO THE Heart Bar Nine and called, "Hello, the house!" He sat his saddle, a staunch, stocky man, with the harsh light of late morning on him. He called again and Lew Case came to the door, pulling on his shirt and with his hair rumpled.

"What'd you want, Hank?"

"Jack Humphries is dead. He's back yonder in the trail, shot to hell."

Lew Case fumbled with his shirt buttons. The shock had driven away his sleep. "You're stuffin' me, ain't you, Hank?"

Hank Davis bristled gruffly. "Why in hell would I be telling you a lie, Case? I was ridin' the hill country looking for Bar Y stock and I almost rode across Humphries' horse in the brush and then I found Humphries."

"What the hell was he doing on Heart Bar Nine land? And who do you reckon killed him?"

Hank Davis spat. "Damned if I'd know and damned if I care. Somebody should've killed him long ago, afore he was born, in fact. Guess we'll just leave him there and tell the coroner down in town."

Lew Case was still a little dazed. He grouped his thoughts slowly, Humphries had been riding home and somebody had ambushed him. Who had done it? He thought of Matt Carlin and Joe Hawkins and Matt's crew. Had one of them notched off Humphries? If so, why?

Or had Humphries run into the rangers and decided to gun it out with them? That didn't seem logical. For that matter, Humphries had had quite a few enemies; any man that had run his trail through life was bound to pick up some deadly enemies—his way of living would determine that.

Maybe one of these had hunted Humphries down and killed him. . . .

" What'd you say, Lew ? "

Lew Case let his thoughts slip away. " Sure, I'll head back for the Bar Y pronto, Hank. Yeah, we better get the wagon decked out for round-up. Was aimin' to ride back this afternoon after I done a few chores around the ranch here."

" Looks to me," said Hank Davis, " like the Bar Y has been losing stock."

" What makes you say that ? "

" There was quite a herd of young stuff and fat heifers back on Antelope. Saw them there the other day, about a week back, I reckon. Couldn't see a track of 'em this morning over that direction."

" They probably wondered back into the brakes," said Lew Case slowly. " We'll dig them out when we start round-up. Unless, of course, this Carlin gent is in cahoots with some border men and is shovin' Bar Y stock across the line into Mexico."

" Kinda a tough accusation, Lew."

Case shrugged. " Could be, Hank." He watched the blocky rancher's seamed face.

Davis was looking off across the distance, the sunlight drawing his craggy brows lower. " They're a hard spread," he finally said. " Well, sling your saddle up and let's hit for home."

" Okay, Hank."

An hour later, they rode down on Cottonwood Creek. Lew Case was doing his best to be congenial, but in spite of his efforts his face was thin, and behind his grey eyes ran the pull and rip of his thoughts. Len Ducom was dead and now Jack Humphries was dead. Matt Carlin had killed Len Ducom, but who had killed Humphries ? Who, he figured, would profit by Humphries' death ?

Behind his bland exterior, Lew Case wrestled with that thought. One by one he placed suspects under a mental questioning and mentally eliminated them. Carlin had killed Ducom but he had not killed Humphries. For what reason would Carlin have had to kill the former Circle W *segundo?*

Only two possible alternatives remained. One suspect was Mack Williams, who had argued once or twice with Humphries; another was Pandrill. Lew Case let his suspicions rest on Williams and then decided the man had not hated Humphries enough to kill him. What, then, about Pandrill?

Pandrill had faith in no man; he had faith only in himself. One less finger in the pie, one less way to cut the pot—with Humphries dead. Lew Case felt a thin chill along his spine. The coldness started at his neck and ran down. And he knew, then, that when he was around Pandrill he would never leave his back to the man.

"Let's ride up to Tumbling Creek," said Hank Davis. "I want to talk to this Carlin gent."

"You might get into trouble."

Hank Davis shrugged. "I don't think so," he said.

When they rode into the yard, they saw that Joyce Davis' pinto was tied to a cottonwood tree. Old Hank's forehead pulled down into a deep scowl and he mumbled something under his breath. Case took in the scene with steady eyes and rubbed his long, thin nose. Matt Carlin had built the place up: the house was almost finished, the location was just right for every building, and the spot was right for the headquarters.

Dippy Bullon was working on the round-up wagon, stringing on the canvas top with the help of Slim Kirkpatrick, and they both stopped and slid to the ground. They stood with their backs against the wagon box and waited and nodded as the two rode by. Hank Davis saw their vigilance and so did Lew Case, and it affected Case the more. This range was going tight and men had their hands close to their guns, and suspicion and danger and darkness were moving across the border air.

Willie Day, who had been squatting beside a small fire heating some horseshoes preparatory to shaping them, got to his feet and nodded, his bare, bald head smooth under the sharp sun. Joe Hawkins was up by the house, and he stopped and stood silent. They rode to where Matt Carlin and Joyce Davis stood beside the new corral.

Hank Davis said, "Morning, Carlin," and Lew Case nodded but was silent. Matt Carlin said, "Howdy gents," and looked at Case, who met his gaze without a sign of emotion.

Hank Davis glanced at his daughter. "You ride far for so early in the day, Joyce."

"The same," said Joyce, "could be said about you, Dad."

Hank Davis' leathery eyes showed anger; then this fell back. Carlin was watching closely and saw that all was not well between this man and his daughter, and Matt Carlin wondered if he had anything to do with inciting this open display of antagonism. Hank Davis looked at Matt.

"You're doing well, Carlin. Just thought we'd ride over and see how things were coming along. Running a wagon out soon, it looks like."

"Hope to. And you?"

"Soon I guess. Few more weeks. Looks to me like I've lost some stock, but a man can't be sure when he runs cattle from here to hell and gone. If we find any Circle W brands across Cottonwood we'll shoo them across, and I hope you do the same with any Bar Y stuff. Or would you want a rep to ride with our wagon?"

"Your word is good," said Matt.

Davis pondered that. He had inside of him a feeling of liking for Matt, and he wondered from where it came and what prompted it. But he had shut himself up for years, keeping his feelings and thoughts to himself, and he had no note of this in his voice.

"It's been good for a number of years, Carlin."

Matt sensed the undertone of gruffness in the cowman's voice. It rankled him, for Davis was deliberately twisting his statement around, making it sound as though Matt distrusted him. Matt felt this edge of anger and then dulled it. He glanced at Lew Case, noticing that the man was light in his saddle, and he had the impression then that Case was stiff inside, that his nerves had brief spots of rawness. He felt a little tired, a little disgusted.

"All right, Davis."

"No reps then," said Hank Davis. He went to turn his horse and then stopped. "We found a dead man this morning south of the Heart Bar Nine. Shot from the trail, it looked like. He was Jack Humphries."

Matt Carlin was silent. Lew Case's eyes were bright on him. Matt knew that Davis had voiced the statement deliberately in an abrupt attempt to catch him off guard. Thus, if Matt had known about Humphries' death he might have momentarily had his defences down and showed this fact.

"Who do you think killed him?"

Davis shrugged. "Don't know, Carlin."

"He had enemies," said Case.

Matt looked at Case carefully. "When a man rides a turning trail the troubles pile up, and enemies come with trouble. The past has a way of stepping up and grabbing a man by his collar and pulling him back."

"My God," said Joyce.

Matt glanced at her. She was bright and warm and her hair was piled-up bronze. She was beautiful and wholesome and she had her attractions. That he could have her when he wanted, he knew. He had an appetite for her but it was not great. She would acquire depth with the next few years, but he had acquired that same depth some years before, and this was a gap dividing them. Their age difference was not too great; in fact, it was not great at all. But his years had been packed and hers had not been hurried.

"We're notifying the coroner," said Davis.

"A busy man lately," said Matt quietly.

"And maybe busy later," said Case.

Matt let that ride. "Maybe so, Case." There would be a time and place for this trouble, and if Case were in it Case would have to pay. Pandrill had his ways, and if he had murdered Jack Humphries that was Pandrill's business and Humphries' business. Both had chosen the same trail. Maybe that trail had hit a fork, and Pandrill had killed Humphries.

He had seen it before.

Davis said, " So long, Carlin," and to Joyce, " Come along, daughter." Joyce glanced at Matt Carlin and lifted her shoulder. " The pater speaks, Mr. Carlin, and the obedient daughter obeys." There was mockery in her tone and a hint of cynicism. She went to her horse and found the oxbow stirrup and turned the beast. " Good-bye, Matt."

Matt said, " Adios, Joyce."

She galloped after her father and Case, catching them when they reached the willows. She looked around and saw that Joe Hawkins had moved over close to Matt, and she lifted her hand, Matt waved back, and then the willows came in and hid him. She put her pinto at a lope beside her father and they ran across the hills and slowed only when they reached Cottonwood Creek, where they watered their horses in the cold, rumbling mountain stream.

Case said, " That water may be a little red some day soon. . . . Blood."

" You talk like a damned fool," snapped Hank Davis. " You been reading some blood and thunder story somewhere ? "

Case's eyes were opaque. He ran his finger along his nose and rubbed. Then he put his horse into the stream and the beast shot spray into the morning air. Hank Davis and his daughter followed, and when they got on the Bar Y side of the stream old Hank said gruffly, " You better not hang around that Carlin fellow, girl ; he's dangerous."

" History repeats itself," sighed Joyce. " You told me once my mother's dad told Mom the same about you."

Hank Davis glanced at her quickly. He had two sudden impressions : she was a woman now, with a woman's burden ; and she had grown away from him, and day by day the differences between them would become greater.

" You'll make your husband's life miserable," he grunted.

FIFTEEN

THERE HAD BEEN LITTLE SLEEP for Marjie Elwood that night. She had seen Dave ride out, dark against the surrounding darkness, and that had driven all sleep from her. She thought at first that she would saddle a horse and follow him, and then she had discarded that thought. Dave would ride a fast trail and a dark one.

She had seen Humphries ride out, too, and after Dave had left, she had seen Mack Williams leave. Zeke Pandrill had already left, and she figured that somewhere the three would meet with somebody. Moreover, she knew this would be with Lew Case at the Heart Bar Nine. She had seen Humphries once, a month or so before, heading through the hills. She had followed him with her glasses and seen him ride into the Heart Bar Nine. She had known, then, that Case was in on this, too, as had been Ducom at that time. The web was tight.

The night dragged on and the crickets chirped. Stillness lay across the peaks and ridges and silence held the inverted bowl of the sky closely against the soil. Finally she saw Dave ride in. He went to the *hacienda* and still she waited, and finally Mack Williams came in and went to the bunkhouse. Dawn was moving across the sky then, filling the dark spots with light, and she remembered the legend of Apollo and his horses, and of the sun-chariot. And now, she thought, Apollo is going out to run the sun across the heavens and he'll be alone up there without troubles. Or do you suppose he has troubles with him and he carries them inside of him as he guides his horses with the reins of fire?

Pandrill rode in.

He was heavy in the saddle and his face was dark. He left his horse at the corral, and the *mozo* took him. He went to the house and shook Dave Elwood awake. Dave looked at him through sleepy, drunken eyes.

"What'd you want, Pandrill?"

"Humphries," said Pandrill. "He's dead, Dave. Somebody's ambushed him. I was heading across the range and I found him."

Dave rolled over. "Where is he now?"

"Left him there."

"What t'hell am I supposed to do?" asked Dave sarcastically. "Stand up and dance a jig or something? He was over twenty-one and knew where the road led." He rolled over and put his back to Pandrill. "Get out and let a white man sleep."

"Who do you suppose killed him?"

"I don't know," said Dave, "and I don't give a damn. Whoever killed him should get bounty money." He started breathing heavily and was soon asleep.

Pandrill leaned back against his chair. He sat there, thick with conjecture and thoughts, and neither was pleasant. Dave Elwood's snoring grew and a great disgust entered the border rider. He took his mind from this and thought of Jack Humphries, who lay out there on the trail without heat or thoughts. Somebody had killed Humphries and had done it with great competence, and he wondered who it was.

Had the rangers met Humphries and crossed him and killed him? No, that was possible, but not probable. He cut them from his suspicions. That left Lew Case and Mack Williams, and he could not see why either would have killed Humphries. Case, of course was out completely: he had been in the house asleep, and Pandrill had been in the next room, and when Pandrill had awakened and left early, Case had still been asleep.

He leaned back, his eyes closed. He thought, Joe Hawkins, he's killed him. . . . He dallied with that and sucked it dry. Hawkins had known many trails and he had crossed Humphries back on one of those trails, and maybe Hawkins had run across him and called him and killed him.

And Hawkins had crossed Mack Williams, too. And, for that matter, he and Case had once been almost at pistols. . . . Pandrill had the impression of horses running away, pounding against the earth and the wind, heading for destruction and death across some cliff. The thing was moving, and moving fast, and he wondered if he would have to kill Joe Hawkins.

He went outside.

Marjie came up. She said, " Is Dave asleep ? "

" Yes."

" Drunk ? "

Pandrill nodded. " Did he ride into Matador last night ? " He wanted to know something, and she gathered this was important to him.

" No, he was home all night."

Pandrill nodded almost idly. A feeling was growing in him, storming the portals of his consciousness, but he held it from his face. " Jack Humphries is dead," he said.

" Who killed him ? "

Pandrill's lips parted. " You have a good mind, woman," he murmured. " Or do you see things you shouldn't see, or do you hold the power to look into men and circumstances ? Now why do you asked if he was killed ? "

" What else waited for him ? "

Pandrill looked at the sky. Finally he brought his eyes back. His voice was quietly deliberate. " Yes, he was killed—from ambush, I guess. I don't know who killed him." His thoughts were bright, quick, trying to feel into hers, but they fell back, their edges blunted. He had the feeling that she was deep and solemn, but that under this lurked running laughter, and that some day a man would come to release this laughter. He wished he could be that man, but he knew he wasn't, and realizing that, he knew he could do nothing about it.

Adios, señorita," he said.

He went to the bunkhouse. Marjie turned, the sunlight quick on her, and went to the barn, where she saddled a line-back buckskin gelding. She went south toward Tumbling

Creek, riding at a running walk, letting the buckskin seek his own trails.

The morning slipped away and became forenoon and the sun lay smoothly across mesas and plateaus. She met Matt Carlin on the rimrock and pulled up and waited. He came at a lope, dust stirring under his sorrel's hoofs.

" You ride fast," she said.

He said simply, " I saw you coming." They were four words—and four only—and yet there was much in them. She was glad of that, and knew that there was a place for her in his life, even though nothing more had been said.

" Round-up ? "

He said, " Looking the land over and seeing where the best spots are to place the wagon. Come along ? "

She nodded.

They rode across the hills, their talk light on the surface, with Matt Carlin feeling the undertone of her troubles. Cattle were wild and ran fast, the *chamiso* rippling behind them. They saw a lobo wolf heading back for the Sangre de Madres. He was moving across the hills, running with the slight wind, running ahead of the wind. His mane was black and he was heavy with a kill he had bolted in a hurry. He hit the timber along the rim of a high peak and fell out of view.

" Knew I should have packed my rifle," said Matt.

" Don't ride without your rifle on this range," she said. His glance was quick and she continued, " Jack Humphries was killed last night."

" I knew that," said Matt Carlin. " Hank Davis found his body over by the Heart Bar Nine. Davis rode by this morning and told me. Maybe I better start carrying my rifle steady. Who do you figure killed Jack Humphries ? "

Her eyes were steady. " My brother, Dave."

Matt studied her. " Why do you say that, Marjie ? "

" He rode out last night, after Humphries and Williams left the ranch. He came in ahead of Williams. Maybe he didn't kill him, but I think he did."

" Why ? "

"He's not so ignorant, Matt. He knows that he's been double-crossed. He has pride, and it's the old Elwood pride—a stubborn, unyielding pride bred into the Elwood's for centuries. Of course, I could be wrong."

"Watch him," said Matt. "And don't tell a soul what you've told me."

"I don't want to be responsible for his death."

They reached Roaring Ridge, where the wind whipped constantly across the rimrock pines, and rode down the slope into the bottomlands. The pitch of the hill, rising behind them, cut them from the wind, and here the sun was warm and good. The day had run past the noon hour.

"I've got lunch in my saddlebags," said Matt. "Let's light here and eat by those springs, Marjie."

"But have you enough for two?"

"I can eat light," said Matt.

He had sandwiches, and they sat under the sandstones, letting the sun's heat penetrate their bones. Matt was quietly reserved, ever conscious of the woman who sat beside him, and ever conscious of her thoughts and fears. She was young and yet she was old; time had moved against her and aged her thoughts, and left her body young. He leaned back against the warm rock and closed his eyes. He let the heat creep through him, feeling its goodness, testing its strength.

He kissed her.

She said, "Matt, please," and he kissed her again. Her lips were moist and warm and the scent of her was clean and healthy. She laid her head back, fitting it into the curve of his shoulder and neck, and closed her eyes. She said, "You shouldn't have done that, Matt."

"And why not?"

"You think of the reasons."

Matt shrugged slightly. "There are some of course, but I guess the biggest, and I don't care to be brutal, is just ourselves. Dave's a man, Marjie, and his way is built for him, and that is beyond you or me."

"Let's not talk," she said.

They were silent then, and finally she slept. Her head

came down lower, spilling her blonde hair across his shoulder, and he felt the mystery and depth of her creep into him, and he liked the emotion. She slept for some time, a deep, meaningless sleep, and the day was warm and calm. Overhead an eagle circled endlessly, its shadow sweeping across the ground, moving across brush and rocks and canyons and hills. Matt watched the circling bird, and saw its wings flutter only once as it coasted with the convection currents of rising air.

She awakened hurriedly. " I've been asleep. Why did you let me———"

" You were tired."

She got to her feet. " We'd better get going, Matt, or people will be saying things, and thinking things." She found her stirrup and held her buckskin, waiting for him to step up, and they rode down the mountain together. The heat was running out with the sun close to the peaks and shadows were gathering along the roots of the lower hills. They rode into the ranch at dusk.

" I'm hungry," she said.

Joe Hawkins took their horses. " Been kinda worried about you, Matt, and more so since I noticed you hadn't toted your rifle along. But I reckon you was in good company. And how are you, Miss Elwood ? "

" Fine, thank you."

" Dippy Bullon is rustling some chuck," said Joe Hawkins. " I'll take your horses, Matt. Better get outside of some steaks."

Matt and Marjie went to the house. Dippy Bullon looked up from the stove, his young-old face flushed with heat. " I'm a hell of a cook, Miss Marjie. You know, I've always figured that a woman makes the best cook. You reckon that's true ? "

" Might be."

" Why not prove it ? "

She put on a flour sack apron. " I'll do just that, Dippy." She belonged there, she thought. And then she burned her thumb on the skillet. " Damn it, anyway."

Dippy grinned. " Why don't you marry her, Matt ? "

SIXTEEN

THEY WERE MOVING THE GUNS through that night, coming from the north with the burro train. The poker game had started at midnight, right after the mules had been grained and fed hay in the barn, and Pandrill played listlessly, letting a few pesos go. He glanced at the alarm clock over a bunk and got up, shoving his chips to the dealer.

"Count me out, Vincent."

"You're ahead," said a half-breed Yaqui. "That why you're quittin', Pandrill?" He laughed without sound.

Pandrill smiled. He counted his change. "Won three *pesos, viente centavos*, Mex. Flip you a peso double or nothing, Vincent."

They flipped. Vincent reached out and took the *dinero* back. "Come again, Zeke, when you have better luck."

Pandrill smiled again, and ran dark eyes around the bunkhouse. Some of the men were asleep, others lying on beds dressed and uncovered by blankets, and one had rolled on his side in his sleep and his pistol had slipped out of its holster. Pandrill crossed the room and stuck the Colt into the holster without awakening the man. Then he went outside.

He was restless. This showed on his broad, heavy face. He tried to hold it inside of him, and he breathed deeply of the cold mountain air, letting the air push his heavy chest wide. The sky was lighting in the east, building streaks across the clouds, and in an hour or two, after this false harbinger of dawn had erased itself from the Arizona sky, the real dawn would come. And he had wanted to be deep in Brush Canyon and close to Mexico when this came.

He sat on the long porch fronting the *hacienda*. A man

came out of the far shadows, moving almost silently, and Pandrill moved around and watched him. Then he recognised Dave Elwood and he drew his hand up.

"That's dangerous, Elwood," he said.

Dave Elwood leaned against an adobe pillar. "Everything's dangerous, Zeke. A man can walk down a sidewalk and hook his heel and stumble and break his neck."

"You talk like a damn fool."

"Maybe I am one."

Pandrill leaned back against a pillar, keeping Dave in the edge of his sight as he rolled a corn-husk cigarette. This man was a riddle to him, he was a clown and a sage, and Pandrill always had the impression that Dave Elwood was making fun of him, laughing silently inside. This angered Pandrill, but he let the thing die.

"They ought to be coming through soon," he said.

Dave Elwood dragged deeply on his cigarette. "Maybe the rangers waylaid them and shot hell out of them." He shrugged. "Not that the world would lose anything, but I would hate to see an innocent jackass stop a bullet meant for a man. And frankly, Pandrill, I don't think much of the scum that rides with you and draws your wages and, to add a little more, I don't think much of you either."

Pandrill said, "I should kill you for that, Elwood."

Elwood's smile was twisted. "You don't dare pull against me, Pandrill. Not at the present time, anyway. Because if you kill me Marjie takes this place and she'll call the rangers in. And next week you've got the biggest shipment of guns and ammunition coming through that you'll ever have. And I happen to know it's your last shipment, too."

Pandrill studied him. "Go on, Elwood."

"You've got it made, Pandrill. You'll settle down on that big *hacienda* and *rancho* in Jalisco province out of Guadalaharja. You've got the money you need. You'll be a big man down there. *Señor Pandrill*. Or will it be *Señor Villa* or *Lopez* or some other common name to hide your true identity?"

Pandrill felt a tug of admiration. "You have good ears,

Elwood, and some of my men must have good tongues to let you know this. What do you intend to do?"

"Maybe nothing."

Pandrill pulled at his cigarette, but the ash had died. He threw it away. He said, "Here comes the burros," and got to his feet. He turned quickly and started to reach, but already Dave Elwood had the ·38 on him.

"You're eyes are poor," said Dave Elwood. "I had this pop gun in my belt all the time. Or weren't you pulling for your gun, Pandrill?"

"Hell of a thing when one of your friends pulls on you," said Pandrill. "Damn it, Dave, we got to stick together or we fall."

"Sounds nice."

The burros were rounding the long hill, the riders on their flanks. Pandrill went to the bunkhouse and hollered inside, "They're here, hombres," and then went to the barn. The incoming burros were in a corral, and they were hurriedly unsaddled and their kaks and burdens were thrown on the fresh burros. This was an old job to these men and they worked smoothly. In a matter of minutes the train was strung out ahead, going toward Brush Canyon.

Pandrill rode up to where Dave Elwood stood on the porch. "You riding with us, Dave?"

Elwood shook his head.

Pandrill turned his horse and rode back to the burros and took the lead. The whole train—men and horses and burros—were indistinct and shaggy shadows in the dull morning darkness. Still Dave Elwood stood there, leaning against the adobe pillar, the ·38 stuck in his belt, watching them leave.

The train moved ahead and the hills reached out, clasping Pandrill and the leaders into their folds, hiding them from Elwood's vision.

The men who had come in with the burros trooped into the cook shack where By Hell had smoke coming from the stovepipe chimney. Dave Elwood went back into the house. There was a jug on the table and he drank from this. He went to the wall rack and got his rifle. He broke the weapon and squinted in at the cartridge in the barrel. He stuck some cartridges in his pocket and glanced around the room and went out the back door, carrying the rifle.

Marjie saw him leave.

She had been watching from her window. The blind was pulled low, but she had pushed the corner aside a little and she had seen him pull the gun on Pandrill. She pulled on her robe and slippers and went out the cabin's rear door. The rocks were rough under her thin soles, but she climbed to the top of a small hill and watched.

Dave had his horse tied in some *chamiso* brush. He went up and rode south, hitting the big sorrel hard with his spurs. He would ride a wild circle and cut in ahead and stop on the brink of Brush Canyon and wait.

She turned and looked at the burros. They were slow beasts, for they were heavily packed, and Dave would have little trouble riding ahead of them. They were far away by now, but the light was brighter and she saw that the closest rider was Mack Williams. Williams was a hard man with a gun and he would see no rangers got on their back-trail.

The burros rolled over a hill and she saw Pandrill. He was heading the outfit, leading the stolen contraband into Mexico. Pandrill was dark in his saddle, and calmly efficient. He swung his mount suddenly and rode back, talking briefly to his men.

"No need to warn you men," he said. "There's rangers on this country and you know it. If trouble starts—or if you see anybody that looks like trouble—shoot first and check up afterwards."

"*Si*, Zeke."

Pandrill turned his horse ; a man rode in. "Seen a rider off to the west," the man said. "Comin' across country from Mexico, it looks like, and headin' north."

Pandrill scowled. "He couldn'ta come from Mexico. He'd of had to come through Brush Canyon." Pandrill put his horse up a slope. He left him behind the sandstones and lay on his belly looking to the west. Sunlight was leafing the range country with shadows and light.

He saw the rider then. The man at least a mile away, but he recognised him as Joe Hawkins. And Pandrill's scowl changed to a dark frown that creased his wide forehead.

He thought, Now what is Hawkins doing on this range? And then he remembered the Circle W line camp around the boggy marshes. Evidently Joe Hawkins had spent the night there and now he was pushing for the home ranch on Tumbling. Pandrill saw the short rider fall out of sight, and he shrugged and rode back.

" See him, Zeke ? "

" A Carlin rider," said Pandrill. He did not add that he had recognised him as Joe Hawkins. " Heading for home." He ran a slow, cautious gaze along the burros, checking the situation, feeling it out and finding nothing alien except his thoughts. " We're getting into Brush Canyon. Push them hard."

He touched his horse and loped ahead, getting the point again. The memory of Joe Hawkins, drifting across the morning hills, lay strong and durable against his memory. He ran this thought through and through and found no menace in it. Hawkins had been going north, heading toward Tumbling Creek—and that was that.

He had not seen Dave Elwood, for Elwood had seen him first. He had seen him as he rode up the hill, and accordingly Elwood had drawn back, putting rocks between himself and Pandrill. He sat saddle quietly, looking down on Pandrill some hundreds of yards below him, and looking at Joe Hawkins heading across the hills. These thoughts registered on him and moved into their proper categories and out of it came one wish : he wanted a drink of whiskey and he wanted it bad.

He had a quart in a saddlebag but he did not touch it. Later, he knew, he would break the seal, but until then he ran the thought out of him. Finally Pandrill fell from sight, and still Dave Elwood was silent, his eyes missing no movement of shadows or sunlight. And when he did ride forward again, he rode fast and with a reckless haste, his rifle bouncing a little in the saddle holster.

Time ran out and moved into eternity, and still he pushed on, riding his spurs. The dark horse let his muscles stretch and sweat ran a fine rim around the headstall and edges of his Navaho saddle blanket. He rode dim trails left by wild cattle and wilder deer, trails that lifted him always higher and higher to the rim of Brush Canyon.

There he found the spot he wanted. The rocks pushed out to the canyon's lip; then distance fell below and into space. Back of these rocks he left his horse, the bridle reins dragging. He pulled the rifle from the boot and wiped it with a bandanna. Again he checked the load and again its contents satisfied him. He ran to the edge of Brush Canyon, then fell on his belly and wormed forward, the rifle stuck out ahead of him.

He was breathing heavily when he reached the rim. He glanced down and saw that the burro train was just rounding a bend a short distance to the north. He wiped his lips with the bandanna and glanced at the blood against the dark red hadkerchief. He coughed a little. lowering his head across his forearm. When he looked up, two red spots glowed on his cheeks.

Men and animals were below him. They were winding along the tortuous trail, and they were tense, alert. Pandrill rode ahead of the lead, riding a quarter-mile ahead, with two riders. Dave Elwood laid his rifle across the ledge, pulled the sights down on Pandrill. Then he raised it again.

"You'll come later, Pandrill," he said.

He let himself grow limp, driving the rigidity out of himself, for he knew it was sapping his strength, pulling dull the edges of his sharp nerves. He let a great calmness come in and possess him. He felt the dryness form across the roof of his mouth, and his throat pulled with the desire for whiskey. He laid his head on his arms and waited, dimly hearing the horses and mules move through the canyon below. The sounds were dull and without meaning. They were empty sounds against the empty void of that primeval wilderness of rock and *chamiso* and eternal peaks with their eternal snows.

He thought, it should be time, now.

Accordingly, he glanced down into the canyon again. The last of the burros were moving under him, going south to Mexico with their guns and ammunition. Riders were pushing the rear laggards. He glanced at them and saw that Mack Williams was not with them, and then he saw Williams some distance behind.

Williams was guarding the rear, watching that point. Dave Elwood waited until the man was below him. He found his sights then; he let them fasten on Williams. There would be commotion below and men hollering, but by that time—by the time they could climb the slope and look for him—he would be gone. This was deep in him, and acid had etched it. But still, inside he was a void. There was no bottom nor sides nor top.

He emptied his rifle.

When he rode into the *hacienda*, the place was silent. Tired men were sleeping in the bunkhouse. Nobody, he thought, will see me ride in. But Marjie saw, because she was still hidden on the hill.

He did not see her.

SEVENTEEN

Lew case left the bar y round-up wagon at Running Mesa and headed for the Heart Bar Nine. He circled the growing beef herd, glancing at the gather as he loped by, and pulled up in front of Hank Davis, who was riding herd.

"Riding over to the Heart Bar Nine for the night, Hank," he said. "Got some chores over there I have to tend to."

"Be back in the morning?"

"Don't intend on staying there," said Case, smiling.

Hank Davis swore. They had had the wagon out for almost three days and things had run against his grain. The gather was too short, far too short. They were getting the usual run of cows and calves, but big steers seemed to be few and a long distance apart, and the Indian agencies needed steers, not cows.

"Be sure you're back come sun-up, Lew," said Hank Davis. "Damn it to hell, where are my steers?"

Lew Case ran a slow glance over the herd. "Quite a few steers in there, Hank," he assured. "We'll hit more of them in a day or two, too, when we work the higher country. Cows stay around water because of their calves, but steers forage plenty wide."

"Hope you're right." Hank Davis glanced at Joyce, who was riding toward him. "Some more trouble coming," he said gruffly.

Lew Case said, "See you come morning," and rode off. He put his horse to a lope, drifting through the gathering night shadows, but he did not ride to the Heart Bar Nine. When he got out of sight he turned toward the south, going toward the Elwood *hacienda*. A few miles from the *hacienda*, he saw two men riding across the hills toward him. He drew his horse in and waited. But they were not Pandrill men. They were strangers to him, and he ran their faces through his brain, trying to place them, but he could not.

One was big with a hawk nose and the other was a thin man. Case rode out of his hiding place in the rocks and they came up to him. He had the impression that they had been watching him all the time and they had seen him ride into the rocks.

He said, " Howdy."

They drew in. The hawk-nosed man murmured, " Hello, fellow," and his eyes were dull. And in their dullness Lew Case read a studied scrutiny. The thin man twisted in leather and looked at him sharply.

" You pick poor hiding places, fellow."

Case said, " You don't know who you'll meet on this range." He was alert and tight. " You men looking for a riding job ? "

" Riding through," the hawk-nosed man said.

Case looked at the brands on their horses. One rode a Slash Six bronc and the other a Smokestack. Case leaned back against his cantle and made his face blank and expressionless, not letting on that those two brands were Mexican irons—that the two outfits concerned raised good horseflesh for men who paid prices for horses that would save their lives by stamina and speed. He had ridden Slash Six and Smokestack horses himself once or twice.

" Good country," said Case, " but there's a little trouble here now."

" No place for me," said the hawk-nosed man.

Case turned his horse and rode west. He reached a piney ridge and looked down ; the pair was heading straight north. Darkness hid them and Case reached the *hacienda* about nine. Pandrill sat on the porch. Case stepped down, leaving his reins dragging. He hunkered with his back against the adobe and built a slow cigarette.

" Well ? " he asked.

" We got the guns through," said Pandrill, " but somebody shot and killed Mack Williams."

Case stroked the match to life against his boot heel. He

let the flame grow and then touched it to the Durham, his eyes sombre behind the scarlet flame. He held it there, drawing deep on the tobacco; then suddenly he ran his thumb across it and killed it. He broke the match and flipped it away.

"Heard about it this afternoon. A fellow came out from Matador with some supplies and he said they had buried Williams yesterday. What happened, Zeke?"

"Somebody on the ridge. Rifle. Williams was behind, riding drag and keeping an eye on the back-trail. Never shot at anybody else. We climbed the ridge, but hell, we were too late."

"Now who would kill him?"

"Why ask me?" demanded Pandrill. What do you say —and why?"

Case was thoughtfully silent. "Could be a number of people. Might even be me, for that matter. I never had much use for Mack Williams. But right off I'd say one name, Joe Hawkins."

"Saw Hawkins that day, too," said Pandrill. He drew on his cigarette and the coal glowed, fell back. "Maybe one of us will have to kill Joe Hawkins."

Case grinned. "It'll have to be you, Zeke. Because I sure don't cotton to no part of Joe Hawkins. You get my cut for that stock that Johnson bought?"

"In the bank at San Ratael. Here's your book." He tossed it to Case, who opened it and studied it, then pocketed it. Case told him about meeting the two riders on the ridge. He described them to Pandrill.

"Harry Perkins and California Ed Dann." The swarthy man considered for a long moment. "Rangers."

Case scowled. "But they didn't hit that gun-train?"

"Maybe they're not so hot on guns," said Pandrill. "Maybe they're just seein' to stopping the cattle stealing we been doing. My men have been working this range pretty good. They've seen them. But they're the only rangers in this locality and two of them can't do much."

Pandrill mused and then talked in a low voice. The

way he figured, Harry Perkins and California Dann would see how things stood, mark the time right, and come in with a body of rangers. They would make one drive and try to get everything at once. Case listened, back to the wall, his eyes lidded. Something was sweeping across this range, something cold and icy and quick—and Case knew that it was death. He was cold across the spine; he shifted his weight to his other leg. He heard boots at the door and looked up at Dave Elwood.

"Howdy, Dave."

Dave Elwood said, "Hello, Case," and nodded at Zeke Pandrill, who nodded back. Elwood was drunk; he balanced himself. "So the rangers are coming in, huh, you contraband sneak thieves. And you're starting to shake a little in your boots." He walked across the porch, not waiting for an answer, and crossed the yard and entered Marjie's cabin. Case was sharp with anger.

"We'll have to kill him, Zeke."

Zeke Pandrill said, "Looks that way." He was tired of Case; he was tired of the trail. He had the thing made, his stake was in the bank, but yet greed held him. One more haul, one more stolen herd. He'd make that, too, and then let the rangers come in—the range would be devoid of him and his men. By then he'd be south of the line, and he'd run his cattle on a range without boundaries. That thought was warm and pleasant and held great promise.

"Two of them gone," said Case. He got to his feet, his spur rowels clanging. "First Humphries and then Williams. Wonder who's doing it and I wonder who's next? *Quien sabe?*"

"Where's Matt Carlin's round-up wagon?"

"On Rush Crick. Why?"

Pandrill had a leg pain; he stretched and lost it. "That means that this end of the range is without Carlin riders. And there must be an easy five hundred head a man could pick up of Carlin cattle and Davis stock. Nice pickings and easy pickings." He showed his restlessness for the first time. "We hit that herd in a few days, Lew. We shove them across and that's all." He spread his stubby, dark hands and looked at his short fingers.

"There won't be no more."

Lew Case felt a push of relief. "All right, Zeke." He turned to leave, halted. "But what about Dave Elwood and his sister? And what if Carlin and Joe Hawkins step in our way?"

Pandrill played ignorant. "Explain yourself."

"Elwood must know about our rustling. So does Marjie. And if Carlin and Hawkins get wise—if Elwood tells them— it means guns. They'll ride against us, and Hank Davis will ride with them."

"I'll handle them," said Pandrill.

Case looked at the dark, squat man and said, "Okay, it'll be your job." He went out into the night and stepped into stirrup. He reined around and looked at Marjie Elwood's cabin. There was a woman in there, a wholesome, clean woman, and he felt suddenly alone, without rank. His trail had cut his life wide and made her impossible, and then he thought of Mexico and women who also had something behind them. They would be as he was, without honour or place, but none of them would mention it; they would only think about it.

He saw her shadow against the blind and he looked at it. He rode out then, heading to the north, drifting with the wind. He thought of Marjie and wondered what she was doing, what she was saying. Had he known the latter he would have solved the riddle surrounding the deaths of Humphries and Williams.

Marjie Elwood said, "So you killed the two of them, then—you killed Humphries and Williams?"

"Why do you say that?"

"I saw you ride out both nights," she said simply.

Dave Elwood got to his feet and crossed the room. He leaned against the mantelpeice over the fireplace and coughed into his handkerchief. His shoulders rocked and Marjie felt the pull of pity. When he looked at her his thin, handsome face showed a whimsical smile.

"Conan Doyle," he said, "shouldn't have wasted his time writing about Sherlock Holmes; he should have known you." He appealed to the surrounding walls. "God in heaven, I hope all women are not as inquisitive, or awake, as you are, Marjie. What hell their husbands would have to live." He spoke to her directly. "All right, we'll say I did kill them. What then?"

"Why did you do it?"

"Why do you think?"

She looked at her fingers. She felt weak, impotent, shaky. The answer was clear to her, and she felt a touch of satisfaction in it. "Pride," she said, "Elwood pride. Your father had it, and beyond him there were his father and endless other generations. It led them all to suffering and indecision; some it led to death."

"They turned our *hacienda* into a house of loot and they broke the Circle W." He silenced her instantly. "Oh, I know what you're going to say, Marjie, and I know you're right. Maybe that's the rub. Maybe I am just a toy Hamlet and maybe I'm walking a thin stage, but the time came when I had to do something." He shrugged. "I don't know why I hooked up with Pandrill. Two reasons, I guess. I'm lazy and I wanted fast money, easy money, and then I figured on drifting south. But Pandrill rode over me, thinking me too ignorant, and that you can't do to a man with any pride."

"And the other?"

He tapped his lungs. "Here."

She was dry inside, and the vacuum was growing. Something would have to move in, to break loose, to flow into this empty spot, to fill it. She knew what he meant: his days were bearing numbers and those numbers were running shorter, and he wanted to taste the high heady wine before he died. But the taste had been fragile and the wine had turned to ashes in his mouth. Now he could not swallow it.

"What is our next move?" she asked.

He stopped, turned, looked at her. "Your next move is with Matt Carlin, Marjie. Hell, I have eyes, girl. He's a man—the only man—and you want him, and he wants you. Go to him."

"And you, Dave?"

He was suddenly angry, suddenly bitter. "Damn it, are we back there again?" Again he appealed to the four walls. "They're all the same. God cut them from the same pattern. What can a man do with them?" His voice fell back and the red spots glowed on his cheeks. "Do you know what Pandrill's next move, and his last move will be?"

"No."

He went to the door and flung it open. He stepped out, closed the door, and she heard him walk around the house. Then the door opened and he came inside. "Sorry; thought maybe somebody was listening." He was himself again and he was cold with indifference. "He'll raid Matt Carlin's herd on this end of the range while Matt and his men are working Rush Creek. There are Davis cows in that bunch, too. He'll haze them through Brush Canyon and into Mexico. And if Matt Carlin or his riders get in the way——"

"Tell Matt," she said.

"And get him killed? When you, my sister, want to spend the rest of her days with him? No, Marjie, you can't live with a dead man. Better to let Pandrill get the cattle and ride them south and disappear into the deserts of Mexico."

"But Humphries and Williams—Zeke Pandrill won't let their deaths ride. No, don't stop me! You know and I know that Pandrill has never felt emotion toward a living thing, except maybe a horse or two. He'll kill the man who killed Humphries and Williams. He won't do it because of the fact he liked the pair; he'll do it because no man can ever say he murdered one of Zeke Pandrill's riders and got away with it. And when he finds out that man is you——" she stopped, became silent.

He waited, but she did not speak. "He'll do what?" he prompted.

"He'll kill you, Dave."

"You only die once. No, that sounds melodramatic. Shakespeare said it, I guess, when he said, ' A coward dies a thousand deaths, but a brave man only dies once.' I know I'm not saying that correctly, but you get the idea. And maybe he won't find out, Marjie."

She shook her head. "He'll find out."

"I want one promise from you. That is, you'll never tell. As long as I'm alive. You promise that?"

She looked at him closely. Some plan was brewing back of his eyes; it was drawing the lids down heavily. She wondered momentarily what it was. She had the feeling that he had shut her out of his thoughts and plans, that he had built his own future and there was no place for her in that future. It was like a cold wind running across the Sangre de Madres, running across the high, cold snows and hitting you when you rode a windy ridge.

The scent of the wild flowers blooming outside her window seeped in and perfumed her room. She heard the bawl of a calf out on the range. Her tongue felt dry and tasteless and she wondered why.

"And I promise that, Dave."

He said, "Have you a bottle of whiskey?"

She went to her cupboard. She took two fragile glasses from it and a pint bottle of whiskey. He poured the drinks, his hands steady, and he handed her a glass. She drank it quickly, revolting at the harshness, and feeling its warmth. She put her glass on the table. He downed his drink, poured another, turned it into him. Then he held the glass between thumb and fingers and his lips were whimsical as though he were smiling at some jest of fate at some inner madness.

"Mother's glasses," he said. "I didn't know you had them, Marjie."

"I saved them."

"She was proud of them," he said. "They came from Spain in the seventeenth century. They've seen a lot of life. They've touched haughty lips, repentant lips, lips without heat." The whiskey, coupled with that he had drunk before, was hot inside him. "Those lips are dead now. Maybe the glass should be broken."

He squeezed the slender stem hard.

"Dave," she said, "don't."

The glass tinkled and shards of it danced across the floor. They lay brittle and sparkling under the lamplight. He dropped the stem and put his hand on his sleeve. He had cut it a little.

"Here, I'll bind that——"

"No," he said. He turned and walked out.

EIGHTEEN

The rush creek range was rough range and made for hard riding and a slow gather. It was a high boulder country with stiff slants and a lot of brush. The cattle were wild and spooky. Matt Carlin pulled his bronc in and grinned at Willie Day.

"Makes a man wish he'd stayed in Texas, Willie," he said. "Back there, when a horse falls, he falls on the level, he trips over something. But here, when he falls he always falls downhill."

Willie Day showed a toothless grin. "This Elwood gent must've crossed these cows with forked lightning, Matt. I saw one that didn't even start to run; she just zoomed off. Take a quarter horse on a smooth track to catch her and turn her. She busted through the brush and headed down-slope with fur flying."

Matt loafed in his saddle, tired and without feeling. Riders were moving across the hills and, despite Willie Day's exaggerations regarding the speed of the Circle W stock, cattle were filling the draw where the herd was being held. They were working the round-up correctly, Matt saw. All the circle riders did was to haze the wild stuff down the slope, where they joined other cattle and drifted down around Rush Springs, where two men held them.

Matt squinted at the afternoon sun. "That's enough for today, Willie." He swung his arm in a great circle. From a far ridge Joe Hawkins saw the signal and his hat swung in reply. Matt and Willie rode toward the springs and Joe joined them at the junction of the coulee.

"Rough cattle, Matt, and rough country."

"They tell me," said Willie, "that they'll not be so damned wild over on the other end of your range, Matt."

"Hank Davis told me the same," said Matt.

Joe Hawkins shoved his hat back and scratched his head. "Saw Hank Davis today. He says his gather is short of beef stuff. This Davis don't seem to be such a bad gent, Matt. Fact is, I sort of like the old devil."

"Headstrong," said Matt. "But all right underneath. Him mentioning his beef stuff is short hits the nail on the head for this gather. Damn it to hell, there ain't many big steers here, Joe."

Joe Hawkins squinted. "I've noticed that." He was studious for a while. "Maybe we'll hit them further back in the hills. Things are shaping up around here and I don't like the looks of them, Matt. Now who in the hell killed Humphries and who killed Williams?"

"Damned if I know, Joe."

"Ambush range," murmured Willie Day. "Ain't a nice chore to ride through the rocks and wonder when and if a slug of lead will come out of nowhere and break your spine. Hell, the signs point to a handful of men, Joe. You never had no admiration for them two; neither did me nor Matt. And there's this Lew Case gent. I don't like the cut of his Levis. But that little red-headed Davis filly sure looks good in a pair of Levis. Now that we're on the subject. Saw her riding off in the distance today, and I sure wish I was about forty years younger."

"Oh, Lord," said Matt, "we're off on that again. Make it sixty years, Willy." He looked toward the round-up herd. "Appears to me we got company."

"Harry Perkins and California Ed Dann," said Joe Hawkins.

The two rangers were seated cross-legged beside the Dutch oven, drinking coffee from tin cups. They exchanged greetings and kept on eating the biscuits that Dippy Bullon was shoving their way. Matt and his men left their horses with dragging reins beside the rope corral and went to where the pair sat.

"What's news?" asked Matt.

Harry Perkins rubbed his hawked nose. "The net's coming in, Matt. They're bunching cattle on your west range, aiming to shove the dogies across the line into old Mexico."

"I'm short-handed," said Matt, "but I guess we'll ride over there with you men. Thirty miles off, though, and by the time we get there——"

Perkins interrupted. "That ain't the game, Matt. Me and California Ed here are playing the game sorta slick, even if I say so myself. We got a ranger company back in the hills. Even now some of our men are watching Pandrill and his renegades work your stock. We're letting them stage the whole thing and then we're coming in and busting them as high as hell. We're letting Pandrill walk into our trap."

"He's smart."

"We'll get him." Perkins drank and said, "How about another biscuit, Dippy?"

"Seems to me," said Dippy, grinning, "that me and you almost met once before, Perkins. Over in Texas. Only my bronc was faster'n your'n."

Perkins smiled widely. "Good biscuits, fellow. No, your cayuse wasn't faster; he was just fresher. But Arizona ain't got no charge against you."

"Maybe I better stay on this range," said Dippy.

"Might be a fair idea." Perkins bit into the biscuit. "You and your hands, I reckon, want to be in on the kill, huh?"

Matt nodded.

Perkins got to his feet. "Might be a day or two, Matt," he said. "We'll let you know." He paused, one boot in stirrup. "Lew Case is in with Pandrill."

"Figured that," said Matt. "Don't let old Hank Davis know about it; he'd go for his iron and Case would kill him."

Perkins mulled that over. "Reckon you're correct," he finally admitted. "And that would make that pretty red-haired daughter of his an orphan. She smiled at me the other day, and for the first time in two weeks I wished I didn't have the woman and the kids. Ride light, fellows."

California Ed glanced at the herd. "You're short-handed," he stated.

Matt said, "Damn short, California."

The two rangers rode across the flat, heading for the hills. Matt and his men ate a hurried meal and went to work on fresh horses. Matt heeled and Joe Hawkins caught by the head and together they dragged the bawling calves up to the branding fire, where Willie Day slapped the Circle W iron on them, earmarked them and castrated the bull calves. Dippy Bullon and Slim Kirkpatrick held the herd while Matt and Joe worked it.

The hours slipped by. The bawling of the calves became mingled with the stench of burning hair and hide. Matt rode carelessly, old to this type of work, to his rope and his horse. The work was automatic with him and he wondered how many herds he and Joe Hawkins had worked before, with him doing the heeling and Joe catching by the head. You laid your loop out there, right ahead of the calf's hind legs, and you held the loop just right for that second, and the calf stuck both hind legs into it.

You snapped the rope in then, jerking up as you pulled, and the noose settled around the baby beef's legs, pinning them and spilling him. Then Joe Hawkins' rope came in, settling around the calf's neck just back of the ears. You took your dallies around the horn, slapped the old mother cow cow hard over the rump with the free end of your hard-twist, and dragged her bawling offspring up to the branding fire.

Automatic work. He had done it in Texas, in old Mexico, in New Mexico. Joe had been with him and they had always roped as a team. There was co-ordination between them, and this was an invisible tie, stronger because of its invisibility.

Dippy Bullon rode up. "Let me and Willie take a whack with our ropes, Matt. A man gets kinda tired riding around a bunch of cattle all day."

"We gotta get this herd worked before dark." Matt squinted at the setting sun. "Okay."

Dippy lifted his hand and Willie Day loped in. Matt

rode out of the herd, coiling his rope, and Joe Hawkins did the same, riding to the other side of the bunch. The cattle had settled down and by now most of the calves bore the big Circle W iron, the brand looking fresh and new against their sleek hair. One cow stood and licked the burned spot on her calf while the calf sucked, his tail swinging as he had his meal.

The evening was quiet, enlivened only by the bawling of the herd, the chirp of a bird in a cottonwood. Matt rode a lazy saddle, letting his horse set its pace, feeling in tune with the land and its mood. Shadows were moving down from the Sangre de Madres, coming across the hills and the pines with incredible swiftness, and already the snow on the high peaks glowed with the red splendour of sunset.

Events had moved rapidly. He had come to this range, and now he was here for good. He pondered on this for a while, wondering what gods, what fate prompted men, shoved them into the paths they took. But the riddle was deep and had no meaning, and he dismissed it again. He seemed easy on the outside, but across him ran a tight, stiff band of restraint. Dave Elwood was in on this, and Dave would have to pay, as every man had to pay. And what would that do to Marjie?

Quietly solemn, Matt viewed this from all angles, and always drew the same summation. Marjie knew all the facts and she knew they would lead to an inevitable denouement for Dave. She had wrestled with them and made a compromise with them, he realized. That thought would sustain her through what lay ahead. . . .

Dippy Bullon rode up, coiling his rope. "We got them all branded, Matt. Guess we might just as well turn the herd loose."

"Haze them to the east," said Matt. "We move the wagon come morning. They'll drift east and when we make our next gather we won't be so apt to pick them up again. Wish we had a few more hands, Dippy."

Dippy's age-old face scowled. "We got all summer," he finally admitted.

Matt nodded and they loped into camp. Darkness was thicker now, and they unrolled tarps and blankets under the wagon and the rocks. Matt smoked his last cigarette for the day, filling his lungs with the cool smoke. The moon was bright and clear, and he closed his eyes and went to sleep.

NINETEEN

PANDRILL LEFT THE *hacienda* at noon. He went first to the camp where his men were working Circle W and Bar Y cattle. They were riding wide circles, working the gullies and draws, and guards were out. One challenged Pandrill, and Pandrill drew in angrily, scowling at the man who came out of the sandstones.

"You know me when you see me, don't you?"

The puncher grinned. "Just scaring you, boss."

"I don't scare," growled Pandrill. "How's the gather coming?"

The ride had been long and Pandrill felt the push of urgency. The rancher was slow in answering, and Pandrill snapped, "Well, damn it, talk!"

"We got quite a few," said the man. "Almost the number you asked for."

"Ride into camp," said Pandrill. "Get the herd moving south. Where's Lew Case?"

"He'll be in tonight."

Pandrill nodded, and asked: "See any sign of the rangers?"

"Nary a sign."

That brought a frown to Pandrill's forehead. "Don't like that," he declared. "I'd rather have them come out in the open once in a while; then a man could see what they were doing. All right; ride in and get the herd going." He studied the sun. "Meet you at the *hacienda*."

"All right, Zeke."

Pandrill reined around and headed east. The end was in sight, and soon he'd be on a new range, but there was still one more chore to tend to. He had mulled this over for some time and finally he had made his decision. He rode at a long lope moving always to the east, letting his horse set its own fast pace. He was in no hurry, but he had a long way to go.

Two hours later he halted on a ridge. The Bar Y round-up wagon was below him, its canvas top white among the shadows. He judged it to be about four miles away. That meant then that Bar Y circle riders were in these hills. He did not want any of them to see him, so he swung the horse and pushed still to the east toward the Circle W camp.

Joyce Davis had seen him. Higher even than Pandrill, she had recognized the man, and conjecture drew a fine line across her high forehead. Something was in the wind, she told herself, or why would Zeke Pandrill be riding toward the Circle W? She waited until he was a mile ahead of her and then she went still higher on the ridges, and rode along them.

She kept the lip of the rimrock between herself and Pandrill, and therefore he did not see her. He was not riding so fast, now; he had his horse at a running walk. And then suddenly he pulled in among the rocks and looked at the Circle W camp. He had a pair of field glasses in his saddlebag and he studied the camp through these. Joyce dismounted, tied her horse in a motte of buckbrush, and crept to the edge of the hills. Lying there, she watched.

Riders were dots across the hills, but despite the distance between her and them she recognised one as Matt Carlin, another as Dippy Bullon, and the closest one as Joe Hawkins. Hawkins was about two miles away. For some time Zeke Pandrill lay there watching Hawkins, and then Pandrill turned his horse and rode back for the hills, circling through the coulees toward Joe Hawkins.

Joyce frowned.

The next time she saw Pandrill, he was on a small butte and Joe Hawkins was about to ride right below him. Joyce thought of screaming but she knew that Hawkins would never hear; the distance was too far. If she had had her rifle she could have sent a shot low and ahead of Hawkins, thereby warning him of his danger—but she didn't have her rifle. And a ·38 bullet, or its report, would not travel that far. She had just to lie there and watch.

Pandrill brought the rifle up slowly. He waited, and Joyce waited. Her blood was thin and somewhere she felt her heart beating, but it didn't seem to be in her breast; it seemed to be in her throat. Time passed—slow time—and still Pandrill waited, and then she saw his rifle puff smoke. They were lazy puffs—three of them—and she saw Joe Hawkins fall from his horse.

Pandrill got to his feet, then. He leaned back against the rocks, stood that way for some time, then went to his horse. He rode south, riding the high, rocky slopes, thereby making tracking difficult. Joyce waited until the dusk and distance claimed him and hid him from her view.

Then she ran to her horse and sent him down the slope. She rode recklessly but she was quiet inside. When she came to the ambush spot she rode into the thick brush. She was saying, "Joe Hawkins, Joe!" and then she saw the spot where he had fallen from his horse, saw the blood in the brush. He had crawled away into the thick undergrowth. She knew now why Pandrill had waited, why he had moved back against the rocks and waited. Pandrill had wondered if Hawkins were dead, but he had been afraid to walk into the brush and make sure.

"Hawkins," she cried, "this is Joyce Davis."

The voice was thin. "This way, girl."

He lay on his belly beside a stub oak. A wistful smile, boyish in pain, showed on his whiskery face. "How did you come to be here, miss?"

"I heard the shots."

"Did you see who shot me?"

She said, "No."

"He got me through the upper chest. Maybe if you can stop the bleeding I can ride. Where's my horse?"

"He's back along the brush. I'll get him, but first I want to look at your chest. Can you sit up?"

"I think so."

Hawkins got his back against a dwarf oak. He smiled a

little wistfully, and she got a sudden glimpse into his loneliness.
" I've read about scenes like this," he said. " Usually the girl rips off her petticoat and binds the wounded gent, but I don't figure you'll have a petticoat with those Levis on."

" It would be rather uncomfortable," said Joyce.

" That would be fun," said Hawkins, " to see the heroine take off her petticoat, but I suppose she hid behind the brush while she did it . . . " His head fell down a little. " Guess I'm pretty weak, Joyce."

" Hush."

He was silent and still as she took off his shirt by slitting it down the back with her pocket knife. She had seen wounds before—wounds on men cut by wire, gored by bulls—but she had never seen a bullet wound. The hole was small and blue and quite a bit of blood had seeped out. She felt a moment of panic and then controlled herself and went to work.

She tore the shirt to strips, jerking at it with strong fingers. She doubled some of it and made two pads and placed these over the points where the bullet had entered and then come out. Holding these with her fingers, she pressed them in and then with her free hand, she bound the strips around Hawkins' chest.

She said, " I think your shoulder is broken."

He nodded.

" I'll get your horse."

She got the horse. The animal was well broken and had been under the saddle for many years. He disliked the scent of blood, but she tied him short to a small sapling. Then she helped Joe Hawkins to his feet. The darkness was thicker now and the man was stronger, and he helped her as she got him into the saddle.

" Hang on now." She advised. " Use both hands."

" We'll make it, miss. I feel stronger now."

She mounted and went close to his horse and took the reins. She dallied them around her saddle horn and rode out of the brush, leading Hawkins' horse. The injured man was stronger, and he essayed a twisted smile.

"Ain't every homely cowpoke that can get rescued by a pretty girl."

"Your boss can't think I'm so pretty."

"He can't see the forest 'cause of the trees," said Hawkins. "'Sides that, he likes 'em a mite older, I reckon." Joe Hawkins studied her momentarily. Maybe it had all been infatuation and she was over it—and maybe she wasn't. "Now me, I like the young ones."

"Oh, you're back on that," said Joyce.

They rode slowly because of Hawkins. Joyce sought the easiest trails, riding down paths left by cattle on their way to the water holes below. Pandrill had shot Hawkins, but Hawkins had not seen his would-be assassin. Only she knew who had ambushed the Circle W rider.

She thought, If I tell Matt Carlin he'll go after Pandrill, and maybe Pandrill will kill him. She decided she would not tell Matt Carlin. She wondered why she had decided on that. Did she still care for him? She asked herself that question. In a way, yes, and in another way, no. He had made his choice and it had not been she. He had chosen Marjie Elwood——

The thought of Marjie brought another thought—a disturbing thought. Pandrill had broken loose all holds, now, Marjie was at the *hacienda* and so was Dave Elwood. The thing was jumbled up and it didn't make sense and the lines wavered. Suddenly a rider, pushing out of the night, saw her and hollered, "Who's goes there?"

She recognised Matt Carlin's voice. "Me, Joyce Davis. And Joe Hawkins. He's been wounded, Matt."

Riders were coming in and men were calling to each other. Matt Carlin was big and broad in the dusk. "Joyce," he said, "what happened?"

She told him.

Willie Day said. "Seein' Joe didn't come in, we set out to look for him." Matt Carlin moved his horse close to Hawkins'. "Joe, damn you, look at me."

"I can see you, you idiot."

Carlin leaned back. "He'll live," he said. "He's

still got his spunk. Joe, did you see who got you?"

"No."

"Lead his horse into camp," said Matt. He got on one side of Joe Hawkins and Willie Day got on the other. They were only a little over a mile from the round-up camp. When they got in Matt took Joe from the saddle and Slim Kirkpatrick helped carry the wounded man to the tarp Dippy Bullon had unrolled under the mess wagon.

"We got to get the doc from town," said Matt Carlin. "Slim, get a fast horse and head in. Joyce, you'll never know what this means to me. I'll never be able to thank you enough."

"I'd do the same for you," she said.

She was smiling and he read behind the smile. She had seen how things were and she had adjusted herself accordingly.

"Oh, you'd even do that, huh? Well, maybe I ought to put you over my knee and do some of the things maybe your dad missed out on doing."

"Try it some time," she said. She mounted and looked down on him. "Now don't do anything foolish, Matt." Her voice was sincere.

He was instantly alert. "You sure you didn't see the gent that shot Joe?"

She made her voice non-committal. "No, I didn't. Well, guess I better ride back to camp, 'cause Dad'll be in an uproar already. He's probably got the whole round-up camp looking for me."

"Dippy can ride back with you," said Matt.

"I'm over twenty-one," she said.

TWENTY

AFTER LEAVING THE CIRCLE W camp, Joyce Davis swung her horse south, riding hard. Moonlight found her on the ridge above the *hacienda*. She dismounted and stood beside the dark oaks, looking at the ranch below. There was only one light and that was in Marjie's cabin.

She went down the slope, leaving her horse on the ridge. She knocked lightly on the cabin's back door.

" Who's there ? " asked Marjie.

" Joyce."

The door opened and Joyce slid inside. Marjie was wearing slippers and a robe. " Why, Joyce," she said, " what brings you here ? "

Joyce Davis' lips showed a faint frown. " We've played marbles together, Marjie, and fought the other tomboys together. But we got something big to fight now. Where's Dave ? "

" He rode out—this evening."

" Pandrill here ? "

" No, all his men are gone. I'm alone." Marjie's blue eyes were openly inquisitive. " Why ask ? "

Joyce said, " Zeke Pandrill ambushed Joe Hawkins, I saw it from the rimrock. No, don't interrupt me. Pandrill knocked Hawkins from his saddle. Hawkins got in the brush. Pandrill was afraid to go in after him. He pulled out and then I rode down and took Hawkins into the Circle W camp."

Marjie was silent. " Did Hawkins recognize Pandrill ? "

" No."

" That means that—did you tell Matt you knew ? "

" No. Matt doesn't know. That's why I came to you, Marjie. He's your man and I thought I'd tell you. Then you can do what you want. Where are Pandrill's men, do you know?"

"They're working the west range. Pandrill is making his last haul. He intends to drive the cattle through soon—maybe tonight."

Joyce asked, "And you didn't tell Matt? Didn't tell him when they were stealing his cattle? What kind of a woman are you, Marjie?"

Marjie sat down. "Why should I tell him, Joyce? This is Pandrill's last drive. He'll go into Mexico and never return. Why should I tell Matt and get Matt and his men to ride with guns against Pandrill and his renegades? What if Matt got killed? No, it would be better to let those border devils get the herd safe into Mexico without gunfire and death."

"But now?"

"I won't tell him."

Joyce said, "Then you'd live with him the rest of your life, and you'd keep your secret in you? What if Joe Hawkins dies? Matt will trail his killer; he won't stay with you. He's a proud man and a hard man. Hawkins is his friend, his only close friend. Do you know men, Marjie?"

"Joyce——"

"That's true," said Joyce. "Every damned word of it." She leaned her head back and her bronze hair tumbled from under her Stetson. "And besides, Pandrill and his riders are stealing Bar Y cattle, too. My cattle. Do you think that will ride with me, with my father?"

"No, I guess not."

"Dress," said Joyce, "and get your horse."

Fifteen minutes later, Joyce was back in the saddle. They swung their horses and rode south, and when they came off the rimrock a man rode out to halt them. Joyce had her ·38 in front of her, Marjie swung her horse to one side, her small pistol in her hand.

"Who are you?"

"Jim Readon, Arizona ranger. I saw you ride in, Miss Joyce. Tried to stop you, but I was too late. We've got the *hacienda* surrounded and one of us was just riding down to warn Miss Marjie, but you beat us to it."

"My brother?" asked Marjie. "Have you seen him?"

"No."

Joyce asked, "And when Pandrill rides in with his stolen herd and his men you intend to jump them? Is that it?"

"That's it."

"My dad would want our Bar Y men in on it."

"They'll be there. We have a man after the crew now. They'll be heading this way, miss. And so will the Circle W men. We sent word to them, too. Pandrill rode to the herd after shooting Joe Hawkins."

Joyce stared. "You saw it, then?"

"One of our men did. He saw you ride down and take Hawkins into the Circle W camp. Then he rode back here. The doctor from Matador was with us in case we needed him. He got the doctor and went to the Circle W camp. You must have missed each other as you rode over here, Miss Joyce."

Joyce turned her horse. "I'm going to ride to meet dad," she said.

Her tone was grave and Marjie felt a sudden emotion. She said huskily, "*Gracias, amigo*, and you'll be with me—at my wedding?"

Joyce said, "I will," and kissed her.

She rode off, and the night swallowed her. Jim Readen moved back into the rocks, and Marjie heard the sound of her horse's hoofs die in the night and become only memories. Things were coming in and coming fast, and she wondered where Dave was. Dave, with his cough, his whiskey breath, and his distaste for life. She smiled, and bitterness tugged the smile away.

She rode north. The moon was high when she met Matt and his riders. She raised her hand high and called to them, and she saw them sheath their guns. Dippy Bullon smiled, his young face heavy with age, and Willie Day showed his toothless grin. Slim Kirkpatrick was silent and the Matador doctor was without words.

"How is Joe?" she asked.

"He'll pull through," said Matt. "We got the Mex goat herd on Wish Crick to get Joe into Matador. Who told you?"

"Joyce Davis. She rode to the *hacienda* after she left you. She saw the man who shot Joe. She didn't want to tell you until she saw me first. Zeke Pandrill shot him."

Matt was quiet for a long moment. "I see," he finally said.

TWENTY-ONE

THEY RODE DOWN ON THE RIM-rock with the moonlight fine and white across the range. *Chamiso* and *manzanita* made dark clumps of wavering darkness on the side hills, and over this the moonlight poured. The high peaks of the Sangre de Madres were white with snow, and on this the moonbeams glistened.

They drew up, deep under the sandstones' shelter, and waited. Jim Readen came out of the darkness on foot and said, " Hello, Matt ; hello, men. How's Joe Hawkins ? "

" He'll live," said Matt.

" The Bar Y men have come in," said Readen. " They're on the opposite side of the hills, hidden there. Waiting for Pandrill and his men to come into the trap."

" They might swing wide of the *hacienda*," said Matt.

Readen shook his head and said, " No, they've got their packs there yet. One of us was down there a couple of minutes ago looking around, and they still had their pack-rolls down there... They'll water the stock at the windmills and then drive through, and that'll be the last Arizon'll see of them—if we let them through, which we won't."

" You don't know where Dave is ? " asked Matt.

Readen shook his head.

" And By Hell ? "

Readen smiled. " We got him out of there some time back. He's back on the rimrock with some of our men. He's got a knife and an old horse-pistol and he's gibbering like a scared monkey."

Matt rolled a smoke. The sandstones shielded the light from below, and he cupped the match in his hands for additional safety. This matter was coming to a head and coming fast and soon it would all be over. Where was Dave Elwood and what was he doing—and after all, what difference did it make? Matt felt a sort of detachment for it all—he was that way in times of crisis. . . .

He asked, " Who's the boss, Readen ? "

" Harry Perkins. Why ? "

" I'd like to talk to him."

Readen went out, and Matt looked at Marjie. She was tired and afraid, and her posture, her eyes, showed these things. He said, " Be strong, girl," and sucked his cigarette. Willie Day had hunkered and his hat was pushed back and the moonlight showed on the edge of his bald head. Slim Kirkpatrick leaned against the sandstone, as did Dippy Bullon. All were silent, for they were thinking of what was ahead.

Readen came up. He said, " Harry's coming."

Matt nodded.

After a while, Harry Perkins came through the shadows on foot, a rifle under his arm. He asked, " What'd you want Matt ? " and glanced at them all, sharply and with appraisal.

Matt asked. " You know about Joe Hawkins, I reckon ? "

" Yes."

" He's my friend," said Matt simply. He searched for the right words. He dropped his cigarette and stepped on it and killed it. " Pandrill shot him from ambush. You've known me for a number of years, Harry. We've got along all right—most of the time. I want you to do just one more favour for me. I want to kill Pandrill because of what he did to Joe. I want to go down there to the *hacienda* and meet Pandrill when he rides in and I want to kill him. Then, when that is over with, and either me or Pandrill is dead, you and your rangers and my men and Davis riders can come in. Will you grant me that ? "

" You talk like a fool," said Perkins.

" That may be," said Matt. " But I asked you a question ; I expect an answer."

A ranger came out of the moonlight and said, " Word's come along, Harry, that Lew Case and Zeke Pandrill are riding ahead of the herd, riding for the *hacienda*. Evidently they're heading in to scout the lay of the land first. They'll be in about ten minutes ahead of the others with the herd."

"All right, Eli."

The ranger moved back and fell out of sight. Perkins looked at Matt and then at Marjie and he spoke to her. "What t'hell do you say, woman?"

Marjie said slowly, "He's his own boss."

Perkins shrugged. "All right with me, then." He moved off to tell his men and get the word round.

Willie Day said, "I'll go with you, Matt."

"Thanks, no."

"All right," said Willie, "you damned fool." He and Slim Kirkpatrick and Dippy Bullon were silent as they nursed their cigarettes. Matt and Marjie moved off to one side and Matt kissed her.

"I'm going to cry," she whispered.

"After I'm gone," he said.

He left her and went down the slope, moving from buckbrush to chamiso and screening his advance. From somewhere to the north came the far away bawling of hurrying cattle, and he stored this impression idly in his mind, knowing then that the herd was close. He came in back of the *hacienda* and went around it to the bunkhouse. He took his time, his muscles a little too tight and his tongue a little too dry, and then he pulled back against the bunkhouse, his gun up and ready.

A man had come out of the shadows in front of that building. He asked, "Who's there?" and Matt saw his gun.

Matt recognized his voice and said, "Matt Carlin, Dave. What the hell you doing here?"

Dave Elwood was breathing heavily. He came in close against Matt and the smell of whiskey was strong. "I made as though I was riding out," he said. "I wanted to scout the proposition. I saw the herd and then I came back to get Marjie out of the way, but she had already left. What are you doing here?"

"Pandrill ambushed Joe Hawkins."

"Kill him?"

"No, he'll live."

Dave Elwood settled back, let his muscles fall out of tension. "They should be coming in soon, Matt," he said quietly. "I think I hear cattle in the distance. This moonlight will make for good shooting." There was a reckless tone in his voice. Matt got the impression that he had pushed himself ahead for this, fortifying himself with whiskey to bolster his courage. "I suppose you'll take Zeke Pandrill?"

"Yes."

Dave Elwood looked at him and then shrugged. "I'd wanted him for myself, but seeing you want him, I'll let him go to you, Matt." His voice was non-committal and without pitch. "Case is with him, and Case tried to gun me down that day you saved my life in Matador. I owe something to you Matt."

"We'll ride out together," said Matt. He was an older person cheering up a younger one, and he saw that Dave Elwood was aware of this. Dave smiled a little and then broke into coughing. He bent his thin body almost double, his mouth buried in his sleeve to gag the coughing sound, and when he finally straightened his eyes were bright under the moonlight.

"Men coming in," he said.

"Two of them," said Matt. "They're riding up to the trough."

There were two sounds. The windmill was turning lazily, its silver blades reflecting moonlight, and the bearing was a little dry—it made a high whining noise. There was this and the push of the night wind across space until it hit the eaves where it sang a tedious song with even tremor. Matt moved to one side and pulled his gun around until he had it in front of him. The handle was straight up, and he put his hand on it, and it was cold.

Pandrill and Case stepped down, leaving their horses at the trough, where the beasts were drinking. Matt was moving to Elwood's right, pushing back against the bunkhouse, and Pandrill and Case came closer. The windmill was humming its shrill tune, and that had a tendency to drown out the song of the wind. Matt waited untill they were almost at the bunkhouse door, and then he said, " Pandrill."

He glanced at Dave Elwood. Elwood was ready.

Pandrill and Case turned and looked toward Matt. Pandrill said, " Who's there ? " and Matt said, " Matt Carlin."

" Step out," said Pandrill, " and tell us what you're doing on the *hacienda* ground."

Matt said, " You ambushed Joe Hawkins."

Case had pulled himself down, and he was dark and quick. There was a muffled, sobbing sound of a man coughing and they turned and looked at Dave Elwood, who was coming out of the shadows.

Case said hoarsely, " We've walked into something, Zeke," and then his gun was talking. The flame was bright and stabbing and it pierced the darkness. The roar of it beat down the whine of the windmill, it smashed aside the song of the wind, for now Dave Elwood was shooting too.

Case was suddenly rigid. He let his gun fall and straightened and stepped forward. He took one step and his knees ran out and he hit the ground on his face. Matt heard the scream of a man above the roar, and he saw that Dave Elwood had pulled back tight against the wall. And Matt knew he had been hit.

Pandrill's gun was out, and Pandrill was shooting. A bullet smashed into the logs beside Matt, and he had his own weapon bucking. He was hot and tough inside ; his gun was a live, bucking thing. He glimpsed Dave Elwood sliding down against the wall, and he heard Elwood holler something, and then he fired his third shot. He had made the other two find Pandrill, and this one hit the man also.

Pandrill said, " Matt, for God's sake. . . . " He turned, and his gun fell. He threw his head back and went sidewise, slowly and steadily, and then he lay down. Matt stood there and waited for a second and he was tight inside. He went to Dave Elwood and looked at him and saw that Dave Elwood was dead.

There was a trace of blood, and a trace of a smile, around Dave Elwood's lips.

The windmill was hissing again, and the sound registered, as did the sibilant purr of the wind in the eaves. Matt backed away, holstering his gun, and then he turned and walked toward the hills. Marjie met him at the edge of the *chamiso*.

Matt lifted his head and listened. " Guns and running cattle," he said.

" The rangers and your men went out to meet the herd," said Marjie. " You aren't hurt, Matt ; tell me you aren't ! God in heaven, if you're hurt. . . . "

" I'm all right. But Dave's dead."

" Dave ? "

" He was there, waiting."

She was silent. Her face was a little too pale. But she had expected something like this for a long time, and expectancy had steeled her nerves. She felt a gush of relief, a surge of renaissance, as though something she had long waited for had come, had happened, and had departed. She leaned back against the sandstones and her hair fell across her shoulders.

" I guess I should cry ; I guess I should weep. But I can't, Matt. He saw his way out, and he took it. Maybe some of the things I said about him were untrue. And Pandrill and Case ? "

" They've stolen their last cow."

She said, " Matt, stand beside me," and he went to her. He put his hands on her shoulders and felt their thinness, and in this he felt strength. " Just stand beside me for a little while, and then I'll be strong again. I'd like to say a million things ; I'd like to tell you how I'll miss him and how much I loved him, I'd like to tell you what you mean to me and what my life means since you've come. . . . " She was smiling then, smiling wistfully, smiling girlishly. " But I can't say a thing, Matt."

" Maybe you don't need to, Marjie." He let his hands fall slowly, moving them across her back, and pulled her slowly to him. He lifted her head and kissed her, and the sweet scent of her hair was in his nostrils as he thought of many things—days to come and years that would slip away into space. . . .